"TRACY! CLINT TRACY!"

He knew that voice. He came to a stop with a wild sense of unreality, a feeling that he had not crossed Utah's miles and Wyoming's at all but was now awakening back in Arizona to find the long trail a dream.

The man who stood waiting was a tall angular shape with a dark, saturnine face that had a perpetual grin. "You don't have to be edgy, *amigo*. Arizona is over and done with."

Tracy took a step toward him.

"This is the way it will be, and I want you to get it straight: I don't know anything about you, and you know less about me. Outside of that, you walk wide of me, Ringo. Because if you don't, I'm going to kill you..."

Other Avon Books by
Norman A. Fox

THE TREMBLING HILLS

Coming Soon

DEAD END TRAIL
NIGHT PASSAGE
RECKONING AT RIMBOW
TALL MAN RIDING

Avon Books are available at special quantity discounts for bulk purchases for sales promotions, premiums, fund raising or educational use. Special books, or book excerpts, can also be created to fit specific needs.

For details write or telephone the office of the Director of Special Markets, Avon Books, Dept. FP, 105 Madison Avenue, New York, New York 10016.

NORMAN A. FOX

STRANGER FROM ARIZONA

AVON
PUBLISHERS OF BARD, CAMELOT, DISCUS AND FLARE BOOKS

This book is based on an earlier story entitled "Winchester Cut."

AVON BOOKS
A division of
The Hearst Corporation
105 Madison Avenue
New York, New York 10016

Copyright © 1951, 1956 by Norman A. Fox
Published by arrangement with Dodd, Mead & Company, Inc.
Library of Congress Catalog Card Number: 56-9755
ISBN: 0-380-70296-7

All rights reserved, which includes the right to reproduce this book or portions thereof in any form whatsoever except as provided by the U.S. Copyright Law. For information address Dodd, Mead & Company, Inc., 79 Madison Avenue, New York, New York 10016.

First Avon Printing: August 1987

AVON TRADEMARK REG. U.S. PAT. OFF. AND IN OTHER COUNTRIES, MARCA REGISTRADA, HECHO EN U.S.A.

Printed in the U.S.A.

K-R 10 9 8 7 6 5 4 3 2 1

For Howdy

CONTENTS

1. The Smell of Trouble — 1
2. At Diamond L — 11
3. Clash by Night — 22
4. The Flickering Flame — 31
5. War Talk — 42
6. Long Stirrup, Sharp Spur — 52
7. The High Hills — 62
8. Hemmed In — 73
9. Hit the Saddle! — 84
10. The One Who Waited — 94
11. Winchester Cut — 105
12. Trail's End — 115
13. Death Comes Riding — 126
14. War at Diamond L — 135
15. Thunder in the Dust — 145
16. Beth — 155

The characters, places, incidents and situations in this book are imaginary and have no relation to any person, place or actual happening.

1. The Smell of Trouble

HE SAW the basin first from a high promontory that gave him a far glimpse of dun grassland and the deeper brown of grazing cattle. In the last sunlight, autumn's haze lay over the land, making all things deceptive. A river sparkled in the immensity below, and ranch smoke lifted here and there like a blue-gray mist, and a town's roofs showed distantly. He had a speculative moment, sitting his saddle and seeing all this, and he let his shoulders sag and crooked one leg around the saddle horn and was at his ease. Then a remembrance of his mission rose and stood stark in his consciousness, and all his thinking harked him back to his yesterdays.

He had come up from Wyoming; and before that, he had crossed the blazing, salt-pocked face of Utah, with the blue of the Wasatch range before him like a beacon. He had ridden in loneliness and liked being alone, finding in solitude a sort of medicine for what ailed him. Before, there had been Arizona. Now, with Arizona alive in his mind again, he had a temptation to turn back, and this temptation was so strong that it hurt him. With great deliberation, he dropped his foot back into the stirrup and jogged his horse onward. The trail dropped, and the basin was lost to his sight, for again the mountains closed him in, old and hoary and everlasting. Timber pressed close, a yellow stand of ponderosa pine, with only the sky open above. But now there was this difference in his riding and in his thinking; he had seen where the end of the long trail lay.

He had traveled light, trusting to such food as he could pack in his saddlebags, that and the hospitality of far-flung ranches and roundup chuck wagons. Some days he had ridden long on a lean belly. He had taken his time. He'd felt rich in time and in nothing else, and the tasks that might need doing at trail's end would still be awaiting him. He had spared his horse; but now he pushed the mount, touched by some impatience that had no name. Thus he blunted a wariness that was usually constant with him. So when he reached a lower level and saw the great boulder beside the trail, he had no knowledge of the one who waited on its farther side until he was looking into the bore of the fellow's rifle. It was the eyes above the rifle that really stopped him.

"You can pile off that horse," he was told, "and unlatch your gun-belt."

Whereupon Clint Tracy, up from Arizona, obeyed, stepping down gingerly. For the one with the rifle was young and his eyes showed fear, which made him twice as dangerous. He stood there, a fuzz-faced range-garbed boy, new to this kind of work and therefore making a great howdy-do of being bitter and brave.

Tracy said, "Easy on that trigger, son."

The boy came forward to pick up Tracy's dropped gun-belt saying harshly, "Step back!" He got the belt looped over his right arm, working awkwardly and letting the rifle waver for a moment. He was a pasty-faced youngster with a slack mouth and the pimples of adolescence. Behind him in the dim recesses of timber, a horse showed. The boy whistled up the horse and got aboard it, draping Tracy's belt over the saddle horn and resting the rifle there.

"Up, you!" he said to Tracy.

Shrugging, Tracy mounted. He might have asked the whys and wherefores, since he was a stranger in a strange land; but a faint, ironic amusement held him silent. He could look upon this boy impersonally, studying his awkwardness as a professional studies a layman; and from such observation came Tracy's still laughter.

The boy raised his voice, saying to the timber on the far side of the trail, "I'll take him in, Snap."

Snap's voice, coming from cover, was an old man's, weary with the ways of youth, holding a mild sarcasm. Snap said, "Shucks, now, I thought maybe you was going to send him in by hisself."

The boy frowned. He would like to fancy himself a hard character and shrewd, Tracy judged, but no man gave him help. He gestured at Tracy with the rifle and said, "Get along, you!" and they began riding on downward over a trail made slippery by a thousand years' fall of pine needles.

Within the hour the country broadened out; and the sun hung low over the western hills, the golden glory of the far aspen fading to blend with the smoky blue of fir and spruce. Tracy's shadow paced him, a long and outlandish thing; and the shadow of the second rider hovered always just behind. Once Tracy got a glimpse of the brand on the boy's horse, an angle with a short line pointed downward at its upper right end. Tracy wondered what this brand was called; it had the look of a gallows. He added this bit to his small store of knowledge concerning Thief River Basin, speculating with only half his mind, for he was biding his time.

As the trail dipped down into a shallow coulee and rose up its far side, Tracy chose his moment.

He was slightly above the boy on the climb when he suddenly neck-reined his mount about. As he crashed his horse against the boy's he saw surprise flare in the boy's eyes, but now Tracy was close enough to let go with his right fist, sledging at the boy's jaw and dumping him from the saddle. At once Tracy flung himself from his horse and upon the boy. Both horses shied, tossing hoofs at the struggling pair, then moved a few steps and stood.

"Damn you!" the boy said, his voice a sob. He said it over and over again, his hands clawing at Tracy. Tracy found him wiry and hard to hold, with the strength of desperation in him; but he got the boy's shoulders pinned down and plucked the gun from the fellow's holster and thrust it into his own pants band. Then he stood up and stepped back from the sprawled boy.

"You made a mistake when you got tired of the weight of your rifle," Tracy said. "When you shoved it into the scabbard, I saw you. I was watching your shadow." He smiled. "Another thing: don't waste your wind cussing a man when you're fighting him. Save it for the work."

The boy looked fierce enough to eat him—fierce and angry and deeply humiliated. He made wild sounds in his throat before the words came. "I'd say you can't be much older than I am. You're a tough jugger, or you wouldn't know all the tricks."

Tracy said with a certain weariness, "I could have got that rifle from you back at the boulder. Easy. You came too close when you reached for my gun-belt. But since there was one of you on that side of the trail, there was likely another across the way. It was your friend had me worried. That fellow Snap."

"Damn you!" the boy said.

Tracy got out the makings and spun up a cigarette. But after he'd touched a match to it, he reconsidered and leaned over and thrust the cigarette between the lips of the fallen boy. "It isn't the end of the world, son," Tracy said gently. "Mind telling why you figured you had to put a rifle on me?"

The boy spat out the cigarette, his eyes still hating Tracy. "You'll get no talk out of me!"

"Where was it we were going?"

"Down a piece."

Tracy smiled. Reaching, he grasped the boy's hand and

hauled him to his feet. "Git along, little dogie," Tracy said. "You first this time. Me second."

He drew the rifle from the boy's saddle scabbard before he let the other mount; and when he'd got his gun-belt latched around his middle again, he herded the boy on ahead of him, a surly, silent prisoner. Soon the hills were an upthrust behind them and a sunset-edged haze to the west. The basin became a rolling immensity all around, broken by low ridges and rising buttes so that Tracy's view never commanded all of it. Now and then they passed cattle, good native stock bearing a Diamond L brand. This Tracy noted with interest, a broad good humor suddenly in him; for though he had never seen the brand before, it was known to him.

When twilight gave way to night, he saw the flickering tongue of a campfire ahead and shortly made out the silhouetted tilts of a chuck wagon and the vague movement of a scattering of horses on pickets nearby. Men sat around that fire, and far out on the plain lay the bulk of a bedded beef gather.

Now Tracy reined short. "This it?"

The boy half-turned in his saddle, showing Tracy a hard face and nodding sullenly.

Tracy took the boy's gun and handed it to him. Then he passed over the rifle, doing this with a smile. "You'll look better packing these when we ride in."

The boy glared at him not being sure how to take this, whether to be grateful for saved face or the more humiliated. At first he said nothing. His mouth worked, and then he said ungraciously, "Thanks."

Tracy counted a dozen men sprawled in the firelight when he and the boy rode into its rim. One of these rose ponderously, looming black against the blaze. There would be a couple more out with the herd, Tracy judged, and perhaps one with the remuda. The fire closed out the night and made of all beyond its circle a mystery.

The big man who had risen peered hard, hunching himself forward. "Who you got there, Herb?"

"A stray rider," the boy said. "He came down through the Notch."

"Why the hell is he still wearing his gun?"

Herb swallowed hard, having his choice between utter honesty and humiliating admission, and made a compromise. "I watched him real close, Luke," he mumbled, not looking straight at Tracy.

"You're a price damn' fool, Herb," the big man said. His voice was impersonal, but Tracy could see that it reached out and touched Herb as a whip might have touched him.

Tracy jogged his horse a few steps forward. "Do I get down, or do we just stand around jawing?"

The big man give him his full appraisal, and Tracy thought: *Too young to be the owner. Riding boss, probably.* There was bulk to this man, and a massive head with a mane of black hair that showed beneath his pushed-back hat, and something else besides, a hard-driving force and an intolerance for lesser men. His face, painted by firelight, was a harsh face; all his features were large except his eyes. He was the kind who rode with a long stirrup and a sharp spur. He gave Tracy a sour smile and said, "You can light if you like." He raised his voice. "Coosie! Company!"

Tinware rattled over by the chuck wagon, and the cook came forward with a cup in his hand and filled this from a coffee pot that had stood by the edge of the fire. Tracy stepped down, standing close to his horse, and took the offered cup. The cook set the pot down at Tracy's feet and then melted back into the darkness. Tracy warmed his hands on the cup and nodded in Herb's direction. "Mebbe so I was mistaken for somebody else?"

"This is a hard country, mister," the big man, Luke, said, no apology in his voice. "We have to be careful."

The smell of trouble hit Tracy then; it was a remembered thing in his nostrils. The boy at the rock with the rifle had merely been a kid doing a job for which he hadn't sufficient experience. This big man was another matter, and so were those about the fire. They had a calculated wariness and a heavy animosity that reached out in the night, touching Tracy like a breath of winter wind.

One, an oldster, thrust a stick into the fire and said, "His saddle is double-rigged, Luke, and that pair of chaps latched on behind is for brush country. I'll bet his ketch rope is a short one that ties instead of dallies. Texas, I'd say. Maybe New Mex or Arizona. He's a helluva long ways from his stamping grounds."

Someone else said, "Pleasant Valley, you reckon?"

Luke nodded. "Old eyes in a young face. A loose way of handling himself like maybe he was afraid of a tap on the shoulder. I think you've pegged him, Cultus."

Tracy remained calm to this being discussed as though he were a rock, but he shifted the coffee cup from his right hand to his left. "I might be looking for a riding job."

"With fighting pay?" Luke asked.

"You hiring?"

"I'm Ramage, foreman."

"I'll do my talking to Cappy Lovett," Tracy said.

Then the smell of trouble became so strong as to choke him. Suspicion rose up from these men and turned almost tangible in the night; every one of them was now his enemy. Even the cook moved up from the chuck wagon and into the firelight again, standing hipshot in his flour-sack apron, standing ready.

Tracy said, "I saw the cattle. Diamond L. Doesn't that make this Lovett's outfit?"

Luke Ramage had turned rigid, but he said evenly, "We're Broken Box. Those are strays we gathered in." He drew a deep breath; he had a massive chest. "There'll be no cutting till the roundup's finished."

Tracy said then, knowing he shouldn't, "A helluva lot of strays, mister!"

Ramage let it pass, but he was still rigid. "You looking for Cappy Lovett?"

"I've heard the name."

The oldster, Cultus, who'd put the stick in the fire, asked, "You maybe a friend of Tripp Lovett's?"

"No," Tracy said.

Ramage waved an arm to the northwest. "Lovett's spread is over that way. It's a long ride on a dark night. He's not hiring. Broken Box is. Stake out your horse and fetch in your blankets. The coosie will fix you something to eat."

Tracy dropped the coffee cup. At the same time, his right hand moved. He got out his gun and held it ready, held it level. In that instant he was aware of every man, where he sat or how he stood; he had measured each of them and pegged Ramage as the most dangerous. He looked at Ramage. "Here's one stray that slips through your net."

Cultus, crouched by the fire, kept his hands carefully before him. "A curly wolf," he said. "Pleasant Valley, sure as hell!"

Ramage was like a rearing grizzly, silhouetted against the fire. Only half his face showed, and his cheeks were hot with temper. "You damn' fool," he said to Tracy. "You're up against more than Herb now!"

Tracy said, "Then it will be hell among the daisies. But when it's over, you can be certain sure there'll be two of us dead. You and me, Ramage."

He looked straight at Ramage and saw grayness come to Ramage's face, but the man's eyes showed not fear so much as a practical man's fight against his own temper and his own strong desire. Tracy held Ramage thus as long as a watch takes to tick, gambling that no man would make a move till Ramage signalled it. Then Tracy stooped quickly and seized the coffee pot at his feet with his left hand. He upended the pot with a turn of his wrist and flung it at the fire. The coffee sloshed out, drenching the fire, and the smoke rose blindingly. Tracy was already leaping aboard his horse. He wheeled the mount about and drove it hard into the darkness.

He expected bullets to come. He looked back, seeing

them all milling about the smoke cloud that had been the fire. He could hear them cursing and shouting. He knew then why they were not at once making their play; he was lost to them in the confusion, and thus his was the moment's advantage. He rode low over the horse's neck, making himself a small target, and he maneuvered the mount along a zig-zag course, glad of the darkness yet knowing it might hold a hundred hidden obstructions.

A bullet came then, not even close. *Herb?* he wondered, knowing how badly Herb was needing to take toll. He pushed harder into the moonless black, keeping to the northwest. He could see the far hills dimly etched, darkness against darkness; and he felt the breeze flowing down from them, cool to his cheek.

After the first mile he pulled up, sitting his saddle and keeping the night, finding in its quiet no comfort and no security. That had been a bad one, that figuring he was in Cappy Lovett's camp because of Lovett's cattle! That's what had come from getting cocky over tangling the twine of the cheap kid.

He stood in his stirrups and listened hard. Presently the basin's floor became a sounding board that brought to him the distant rataplan of riders; and he knew then they were out yonder, making their search. They had the advantage of knowing the terrain, and they were many. He wasted precious seconds here, sorting out sounds until he could make some kind of pattern of them. When it was his judgment that Broken Box had spread out a wide fan of riders, he used his spurs again.

Now his first real fear touched him; there'd been no time for fear in Broken Box's camp. He could only thunder along, wary of the hidden coulee, the unseen gopher hole. Each time he paused to listen, the riders were off yonder in the night, nearer, it seemed. He grew mindful of all the miles his horse had covered in past days, for Broken Box would have fresh mounts from its remuda. His own tiredness took a toll as well; he had been early in the saddle that day. He became like a man moving through a nightmare, conscious of pursuit and trying frantically to elude pursuit, running blind through a blind world, getting nowhere.

He smelled the river before he saw the fringing willows that marched along it, a black palisade. This would be the Thief, which gave the basin its name. He began following the Thief because there was no other choice for him. Ramage's riders had boxed him up. Sometimes he looked out upon the river's dark surface, seeking a ford. The river looked cold and deep and treacherous. He had no way of knowing whether Diamond L lay on the far bank, nor could he tell where a crossing might be the least dangerous. The river was a barrier, and he had either to risk the water or turn back toward Broken Box. This realization put panic in him.

Again he paused to listen. There was movement in the night, faint and cautious and intangible; and he realized that Broken Box must have made better use of this last hour than he. There were closer, much closer; they were all around him. No longer were they running their horses, for now they were drawing tight the net they had spread.

For a moment he was certain that at least one rider was almost upon him; he strained his ears and waited endlessly for some betraying sound. Then he heard it, the jingle of a bit chain. He turned his horse about and drove at the river and splashed into it. There was no choice now. He was a dozen feet out from shore and feeling the tug of the current when the gun spoke.

He judged that the one who'd fired was up there on the bank he'd just quitted, but he couldn't be sure. The gunflame was a flash of brightness in the night, and something exploded against Tracy, lifting him from the saddle. He had a moment that was both a brief hurt and an endlessness of agony before the river claimed him.

2. At Diamond L

HE HAD no remembrance of grasping at anything, but afterwards, when the shock of cold water brought him to partial consciousness, he found himself clinging to a stirrup. The easiest thing seemed to be to hang on and let the horse do the swimming—the easiest thing and the most important. Tracy was mindful of that gunman on the Thief's bank, but the river was his real enemy now. He was a dry-country man with no great experience with rivers and no trust in them; and this river was a giant's hand, dragging at him, pulling relentlessly; the river was a roar in his ears.

He saw looming blackness ahead and hoped desperately that it was the far bank. Then he saw that it was a rock, and horror engulfed him. He let go of the stirrup, not meaning to, and at once he went down, dropping through the strangling depths until his feet touched bottom.

He flailed his legs feebly, a vast, blinding light growing inside his skull, and rose to suck in air. He started going down again and fought against this. He careened toward something and thought it was the rock and tried to find the strength to brace himself for the impact. Then he realized dimly that some whim of the current had brought him up against the horse. He clutched at the mount and got hold of its tail. He clung grimly; he had one thought, and only one: he must hang onto the horse no matter what. The river had nearly done for him, and the river was not yet bested.

After a great length of time his knees scraped gravel. The horse humped up over a bank, dragging Tracy through tall grass and sand and rocks; and he let go then and sank into a second oblivion.

The stars were out and wheeling above him when he again opened his eyes, and at first he merely lay, feeling kitten-weak and having a time placing where he was and how he had come to be here. His thinking was slow, his body sluggish. His clothes were nearly dry. When he got propped on an elbow, he found that his left shoulder pained him and his shirt was heavy with blood.

He looked for his horse and had a panicky moment, thinking the horse was gone; but he found the mount standing nearby. He thought: *Good old boy!* and tried to come to a stand. He crawled toward the horse and reached again for the stirrup. It seemed to be eight feet above him, but he managed to get hold of it, and after a mighty effort he got himself on his legs. He stood leaning against the horse, then made it up to the saddle, where he reeled, clutching the horn.

He looked back toward the river; distance made it seem placid. He tried listening for any sound that might carry above the river's voice; he looked for shapes that didn't belong to the willows. He judged then that he had taken Broken Box off his tail; likely they had counted him dead when he'd gone into the water, and the moonless dark had covered his escape.

He turned the mount to the northwest again, though he couldn't have said why he chose that direction. After a while he remembered that that fellow Ramage had waved to the northwest when he'd spoken of the whereabouts of Diamond L. He shook his head, not wanting to think of Ramage. He wondered how long he could stay in the saddle. A sense of great danger was still upon him, but the danger now was his wound and his weakness. Nothing had ever left him with such a hollowed-out feeling as that bout with the river.

He moved across a world that was sometimes startling in its clarity and sometimes a woolly fuzziness in which he rode by instinct. Presently he saw a distant light and tried to make toward it. Sometimes the light was lost to him behind trees. Whenever the fuzziness came, the light turned as elusive in his mind as it was in actuality; and he was hard put to remember what he was seeking. The breeze pressed his damp clothes against him and made his teeth rattle. His blood had been thinned down by Arizona, and he felt the cold keenly. He tried to get a cigarette shaped up, but the makings were a sodden mass and he flung them away.

After a while he just rode, letting the horse pick its own way and its own pace. When ranch buildings loomed before him, a shapeless huddle, he looked at them in some surprise, wondering why they were supposed to be important to him.

He was swaying in the saddle. He knew that a dog was barking its greeting; he wished the dog wouldn't be so damn' noisy. He had a glimpse of a door flung open and saw a man's heavy-shouldered shape briefly silhouetted against that yellow rectangle of lamplight. Another slighter form crowded beside the man's, and a startled cry was in Tracy's ears when oblivion again overtook him...

He opened his eyes to daylight and the strangeness of a roof over him and a bed under him. He eased down in the bed, liking its softness. He had been stripped naked, and the discovery brought him a hazy recollection of a man's rough hands on him. But it was a girl who came across the room and stood looking at him. She was tall, and her hair was the color of ripened wheat. He stared at her; she was pretty, but she was more than that; there was strength in her, and goodness. These things he sensed at once; and again remembering his mission, he was glad for being here.

She asked, "How do you feel?" then put her hand to his forehead and said, "No fever, thank heavens." Her touch was cool and impersonal, and she had that sort of air about her, closing him out.

Tracy asked, "Is this tomorrow?"

She smiled slightly. Her eyes were blue, and her smile warmed them. "It was last night you stumbled in here, if that's what you mean."

"Diamond L?"

She nodded and left him, and at once he felt his aloneness. He looked about; he was in the bedroom of a ranchhouse that seemed old and solid and comfortable. The strangest thing was being under a roof; he had bedded beneath the sky a long, long time. The girl came back with a bowl of soup and a spoon and took a chair by the bedside; but Tracy said, "I can manage," and took the soup from her. His shoulder, he discovered, was bandaged; and he spoke of this. "How bad?" he asked.

"A deep groove," she said. "The lead winged on, so we didn't have to do any digging, but you must have bled a lot. You had quite a fever when you came in."

He could remember it all—the chase, and the rider who'd got him from the river bank, and that nightmare crossing, and the ride afterward. It was like a dream remembered, but the reality was in that bandaged wound. He said, "I must have been a lot trouble to you."

The girl said, "You did your share of babbling. Something about Pleasant Valley and a feud between a Tewksbury outfit and some people named Graham. We've heard about that up here in Montana."

He was instantly on guard, wondering if he'd told everything. He studied her face for a moment. "Sheep and cattle trouble down in Arizona," he said. "It was quite a ruckus while it lasted." Again he searched her face. Her eyes, he decided, were the most expressive ones he'd ever seen; yet her eyes told him nothing. He said then, "I rode for one of the outfits."

"A hired gunman?"

He tried to shrug. "Whatever happened to be in the day's work."

A man came into the bedroom then, soft stepping; and because this was Diamond L, Tracy judged him to be Cappy Lovett and gave him his full appraisal, seeing a little man, silver haired and mild eyed and older than his years, which were considerable. He wore range garb, but he had a little too much belly for a man who kept up his riding, and he walked with a slight limp. About him there was the patient tiredness of one who had lived so many years that he had made his own compromise with living and convinced himself that the compromise was good. His were not the heavy shoulders of the man who had come first to the doorway last night. He said in a gentle voice, "Able to take nourishment, cowboy?"

Tracy smiled. "You can fry a steak for me come supper time."

"I looked over your gear this morning," Lovett said. "Texas?"

Tracy shook his head. "Arizona," he said and knew then that Lovett hadn't been around when he'd done his feverish babbling.

Some expectancy in Lovett died, and he was an old man burdened with his years. His eyes moved to the girl. "I'll be out on the gallery, Beth, if you need me." He turned back through the doorway, lurching a little. Seeing this and remembering a slight thickness of tongue in Lovett's speech, Tracy thought in surprise: *He's damn' near drunk!*

The girl, Beth Lovett, said, "Do you think you could eat something solid?"

Tracy spied his clothes laid upon a chair. "I reckon I could get up and get dressed."

"Sure you're strong enough?"

"Only one way to find out," he said.

But when she left the room, he didn't try to get out of

bed. It was much easier just to lie there, and presently he dozed. He came out of sleep a great deal later, brought awake by the sound of voices. Seeing the slant of the sun through the bedroom window, he realized that it must now be late afternoon. It was a troubled awakening that brought him some vague sense of alarm and an instinctive wariness. Beth Lovett was talking in a room beyond this bedroom. Her voice came to him clearly; it was edged with anger. He wondered if that was what had awakened him.

She was saying, "If you're just paying a friendly call, Hap, you're welcome to stay for supper. But you've done a lot of empty talking. If you're here as sheriff, to wait around for Johnny, you're just wasting your time. He hasn't showed home for nearly a week now."

The sheriff, Hap, said soothingly, "Now, Beth, this ain't to my liking."

"Then why are you here?"

"Just put yourself in my place. You can hear a pin drop in Spurlock these days. Everybody stands around with a long face waiting for Doc Smeed to show himself with the latest word. Hugh McCoy's making a fight for it up there in Doc's office; but if he dies, it's murder. That brother of yours shouldn't have lit out, girl."

You could picture a man from his voice, Tracy reflected, and sometimes you'd be right and sometimes you'd be wrong. Hap had a big-bodied sound, but there'd likely be flabbiness to him. Tracy guessed that here was a political fence-straddler who'd walked wide of trouble most of his days.

Beth said, "Johnny's running doesn't prove anything except that he's scared!"

"*Somebody* drygulched Hugh," the sheriff said wearily. "You know there's been bad blood between Broken Box and Diamond L for near a year now. Then Johnny up and shakes the dust. How is it bound to look?"

"I'll admit Johnny was mouthy," Beth said. "He told Hugh McCoy once in Spurlock that if Tripp didn't come home and straighten things out, he, Johnny, would do it for him. I suppose a dozen people heard Johnny. When the word came that Broken Box's boss had been cut down from cover, Johnny knew how that would look for Diamond L. Who else but Johnny would have the finger pointed at him? Dad? He hasn't been out of our front yard for over six months! Corb? He's loyal, but he wouldn't turn bushwhacker."

The sheriff sighed. "It's a hard row for me. We're all three of us old timers, me and Cappy Lovett and Hugh McCoy. We saw this basin grow up. Time was when all three of us fought together and frolicked together. No matter how I turn, I'm against a friend. This just ain't to my liking."

"Then wait till Hugh McCoy dies—if he does," Beth said. "After that, you can show up with a warrant with Johnny's name on it. Don't come snooping meantime, Hap. Diamond L doesn't like it."

Tracy thought: *Good girl!* and then he stiffened, for the sheriff said, "Horse in your corral with a brand I never saw before."

"A stranger from Arizona," Beth said.

The sheriff sighed again. "When strangers start drifting in, it usually means somebody sent for 'em. Diamond L importing gunmen?"

Beth said, "We'll stomp our own varmints."

Hap said, "I only asked. Talk has it that Diamond L's apt to be making a Winchester cut of Broken Box's roundup herd one of these days. I wouldn't want to see that happen, not with things as touchy as they are."

Beth said, "Be sure of one thing, Hap: If we go over there with guns, they won't be imported guns."

Tracy heard a chair scrape. There was further talk, but it grew dim with distance, and he guessed that both the sheriff and Beth Lovett had moved on out to the gallery. Presently a horseman crossed the yard beyond the bedroom window, a huge, grizzled man who sat his saddle sloppily, as though he were more used to a swivel chair. That, Tracy judged, just about had to be Hap.

He flung the blankets back and swung his legs to the floor and got to a stand. He felt fine, though he had a stiffness in his shoulder. He got into his clothes. His shirt was a rag; it had been cut away from him last night, but he put it on anyway. He latched on his gun-belt and lifted his gun from leather and looked at it.

Beth came in. "Corb Blount cleaned up your gun and oiled it," she said. "You seem to have gone swimming with your hardware on."

"Blount?"

"Corb's our foreman; he gave me a hand with you last night." She looked at Tracy's shirt. "I'll get you another." She left and returned with one in her hand. "This may be a little small for you."

He took the shirt, guessing it was Johnny's; and when Beth had left, he got into it. He came out of the bedroom and found himself in the ranch-house parlor. Here Beth and the sheriff had done most of their talking. The room had an ancient respectability to it, with a cut-glass trimmed ceiling lamp, a green plush chair, a Franklin stove, and an organ. On the wall were two framed pictures, crayon portraits, one showing a younger Cappy Lovett in a Confederate captain's uniform, the other a woman with Beth's own expressive eyes. He stood for a moment studying the pictures. The strength, he decided, had been in Beth's mother; she had a firm chin.

Tracy crossed the room to a hallway that led him to the gallery, and here Cappy Lovett sat in the last of the daylight, a whiskey jug to one side of his chair, a huge brass-bound telescope lying across his lap. He sat hunched down in the chair, his blue-veined hands on the telescope, his eyes dreamy. He smiled a gentle smile at Tracy and said, "Glad to see you on your feet."

"That's quite a spyglass you've got there."

Lovett nodded, "I've been looking toward the Notch. My older boy, Tripp, is due home any day."

Tracy said, making a movement of his hands, "I'm obliged to Diamond L."

"Arizona it was, you said. You know Texas, too?"

"I've been there. It's a lot of country."

"You wouldn't maybe have met my boy Tripp somewhere down there?"

Tracy said stiffly, "I've met a lot of them."

"A big fellow, Tripp. His mother's menfolks were all raw-boned, and Tripp favored that side in his build. But he's a lot like me. You'd remember Tripp if you crossed trails with him. Folks always remember Tripp."

"Which way is Spurlock?" Tracy asked.

Lovett waved his hand vaguely to the north. Now he seemed really to see Tracy for the first time. "Would you like to hire on here?"

Tracy said, "Sure. Why not?"

And then, because he wanted to get away from this old man who lived out his days with his telescope and his whiskey jug and his hope, he went down into the yard. Diamond L had been built of square-faced log and clapboard; the bunk-house was newer than the house. Beside the barn was the corral. His own horse stood patiently in the corral, and his gear was slung over one of the rails. He walked toward the corral, feeling steady. He unconsciously raised his hand to a pocket of the borrowed shirt and found a sack of tobacco there. He remembered throwing away his own last night and thanked Beth in his mind.

When he raised his eyes from the cigarette he'd spun, he saw a man come from the bunkhouse and cross toward him. The fellow was in his late forties, and he had a Puritan's stern, uncompromising face beneath his Stetson. His body was long and big boned, but the saddle had trimmed him lean. His shoulders were heavy, and by this token Tracy knew him to be Corb Blount, Diamond L's foreman, he of the ready hands last night and the thoughtfulness toward another man's gun.

Tracy got the tobacco fired and said, "I seem to be obliged to you."

Blount said, "Any man with Broken Box on his tail is Diamond L's friend."

Tracy's surprise must have showed, for Blount gave him a thin, cold smile. "You talked some when I was getting your clothes off you."

"Names?" Tracy asked.

"Luke Ramage's. That's all I needed to hear. After that you fancied yourself back in Arizona. There was mention of the Grahams and the Tewksburys."

"My own name is Clint Tracy. Or did you find that out for yourself?"

"If I had, I'd still have been waiting to see if you'd say it."

A hard man, Tracy decided, and wondered whether he liked this Corb Blount. There seemed to be little imagination in the fellow, and less humor. Yet he owed Blount something, and he was remembering that; so he said, "My name's no secret."

"Beth's looking for you," Blount said, nodding toward the house. He moved on, walking neither fast nor slow, and disappeared into the barn.

Tracy stood waiting till the girl came up to him. She asked, "Wouldn't you like some supper?"

"I'll get a bite in town."

"Feel well enough to ride?"

He let the cigarette drop to the ground and set his heel upon it. "I'd like a look at Spurlock," he said. "After that, I'll be back. Your dad signed me on."

She stood there steadfast for a moment, and then her eyes dropped and she traced an obscure pattern upon the ground with the toe of her boot. This was the first time he'd seen a lack of surety in her, and it surprised him. She said, "You were in pretty bad shape when you got here last night."

"I know," he said and touched his hand to his wounded shoulder. "I'm obliged."

She raised her eyes to him again and shook her head. "You owe Diamond L nothing. What I have to ask is a favor, not a reward."

"You name it."

"Ride out of here," she said.

He turned this over in his mind, not finding any sense to it. He was thinking of how many pieces of a pattern he had picked up in his one day in the basin. There were two old outfits, big outfits, and they were Broken Box and Diamond L. There was trouble between them; he had seen Diamond L cows on Broken Box graze and heard talk of a Winchester cut. Moreover, a man lay dying in Spurlock, and a boy stayed hidden in the hills. Always there was something like that; it had been sheep and cattle in Pleasant Valley. Here it was another thing; but always it got down to the grass, the bitter graze that was a cattleman's wealth— and his curse when covetousness overcame him. That made Diamond L in need of a Clint Tracy. The only strength he had seen here was Beth Lovett's, and the only practicality, if he discounted Corb Blount's, who was a hired hand. Yet she was sending him away.

He shook his head. "Your father has hired me."

"Then it has to stand," she said solemnly. "I would not override him in any matter that made him less a man by having to bow to me. But you could go tell him that you've changed your mind."

All the miles from Arizona he had brought with him his secret; and it was a curse upon him at this moment. But it left him no choice. He had made his decision at the Notch, when he had known temptations, yet not turned back. He picked his bridle from the corral rail and put his hand to the gate. "I'll be back from Spurlock," he said. "After that, I'm staying."

He wished he had words to soften this. But none came to him, so he turned away from her and went into the corral.

3. Clash by Night

BETH LOVETT, watching Tracy ride out of Diamond L's yard, was both puzzled and angry, remembering Tracy's stubbornness and the blunt manner in which he had turned her wish aside. She guessed she had expected something different. She had used no coquetry in her approach to him; she wouldn't have known how. She had never schooled herself in the downcast eye, the appealing smile; yet she had been a woman making a request of a man, and she'd supposed that would count. But he had turned blind eyes upon her, sensing nothing but a will opposed to his own. Her bewilderment grew from the sorry knowledge that it was ever thus.

She had known few men other than her father and her brothers and Corb Blount and the crew that rode for the ranch. To each of them she bore a different relationship, but always it was man to man. She had her femininity, but it was a choked flower on Diamond L. She was brother to her brothers and a third son to her father, and something more than that of late, something of a leaning post as the winds grew strong.

No man had ever come courting her; but she had never

wondered about that, not till now. Was it because she'd met all men as equals or something less, finding them a poor lot with their petty squabbles and small vanities? Was it because she had talked to them in their own language and shown no need for the only kind of strength they had to offer? After all, what she had asked of Clint Tracy was that he go his way. And so he had talked to her as one man talks to another; and remembering this, his words and his tone of voice, she found the core of her anger.

He was a dark one, this Tracy, and in his fever he had babbled of a far range and of blood and death. Thus he had touched a secret fear in her, a fear that was entirely feminine, one she had kept hidden. Still she had been drawn to Tracy so strongly that she'd fought not to show her interest when sanity and consciousness had returned to him. Tonight she had told him that she asked no reward; yet she had expected any woman's reward, the chivalrous word, the gracious gesture. These he had denied her. And now her anger faded when she recalled how forthright his denial had been.

But the secret fear was still hers, the fear that been growing for over a year now; and it brought her a reminder of a task to be done. No sense standing here mooning about a man!

Turning, she crossed the yard to the house, passing her father wordlessly and going into the kitchen. Here she stood for a moment. This kitchen was one part of Diamond L that was predominantly hers. Here her womanliness displayed itself in neatness and gay curtains, the choked flower fighting the cramped earth of man's domain.

She had her solitary moment of belonging to the kitchen, then stirred herself and began rummaging about. She found a nearly empty flour sack and spilled its contents into a bin. Then she stuffed dried apricots and canned tomatoes into the sack, adding a supply of ground coffee and a slab of bacon and a loaf of bread she had baked only the day before. She worked swiftly.

In the course of her search for food, she found hidden

away in one of the cupboards a whiskey jug. This was her fathers. She sloshed it to estimate its contents, then added a dipperful of water from the kitchen pail. She had never reprimanded Cappy Lovett for his drinking; but she had often used this method of cutting his liquor, hating her own sly way but choosing it in preference to the edged remark, the steady nagging.

The grub sack filled, she took it through the kitchen door and came the long way around the house to the corral. Twilight softened the yard. Horses stomped in the corral, the dog slept curled beside the well, and the hills beyond lay in quiet glory. She liked this hour for its serenity. Light had not yet sprung from the bunkhouse windows, but she judged that the crew was inside. Only Corb Blount showed in the yard. He was seated on the bench beside the bunkhouse, carefully cleaning his Winchester, the rifle across his lap, the wiping rag in his hand.

Beth set the grub sack beside the corral gate, lifted a rope from a gate post, and laid a loop on her private saddle horse, a buckskin mare. Blount looked up, his stern face asking her if she needed help. Beth shook her head and did her own saddling quickly. She had hoisted the grub sack to the saddle horn and tied it there and was rising to the leather when Blount came across the distance between them, the Winchester under his arm.

He stood at her stirrup, a tall, unsmiling man, his face wooden. He had always shown her a quiet respect that was part of his deep loyalty to Diamond L, and his voice now held that respect. He said, "Elizabeth, I have scouted again. I had no order not to do so. There are more Diamond L cattle in Broken Box's gather."

"I know, Corb," she said.

He looked to the southeast, his eyes suddenly hard. He might have been a circling eagle seeing all the land. "How long?" he asked.

She was touched by the torment in him, but she said, "My father is the boss of Diamond L."

He nodded. "Cappy Lovett waits for Tripp. But sometimes I think Tripp will never return. I dream of Tripp often, and he is always a shadow in my dreams, and no man gets a hold on him. We cannot keep waiting."

He moved the Winchester into his hands and worked the lever, the sound harsh in the dusk.

Beth cried, "No, Corb! Not as long as any other way is left!"

He said gravely, "I would have to have my orders. Do not think that I am forgetting that."

"We'll talk about it tomorrow, Corb."

He looked at the grub sack. She had moved it through the kitchen doorway to keep it from her father's sight, but she had long ago learned that there was no keeping a secret from Corb Blount. He nodded toward the sack. "Tell him that no harm will come to him," he said. "Not unless he goes seeking harm."

This startled her; and she asked, "How could you know that?"

He merely shook his head, and the gesture closed her out. He had always been a strange man, given to his own solitary thoughts and his own queer ways. He had been with Diamond L as long as she could remember, and she heard it hinted that he was part Indian, though he was like no Indian she had ever known, no Montana Indian. Once she had seen a picture of an Aztec, though, and it had reminded her of Corb Blount. He kept a dream book in the bunkhouse—he made no secret of this—and he counted strongly upon all the portents. She supposed now that he was making reference to something that had meaning only to himself, and therefore she did not press him.

She was growing impatient, mindful of the task to be done; so she murmured, "I'll tell Johnny what you said," and, lifting the reins of her horse, rode out of the yard.

Her trail took her northeast to a ford of the Thief, and she crossed a placid river that looked little like the wild one Clint Tracy had swum. Thereafter she rode almost due east, her eyes alert; for though the sun was gone behind the hills, there was still light enough to see and be seen.

She got to thinking about Clint Tracy again, recalling how she had mothered him last night; and it came to her that she mothered all of them, even her own father. She had never thought of this before, and she supposed that it explained many things. She remembered dances where other girls clung to men or made soft laughter in the night, out where the buggies and buckboards were gathered, while she sat on a wall bench awaiting the dutiful courtesy of her brothers and the Diamond L crew. She had never had time to be a girl; she had been self-reliant and more than that.

Thinking thus, she rebelled against Diamond L; she felt strangled by all the responsibility she'd had to assume. Tonight, for instance. Yet even now she was seeking out a certain landmark; and she came upon it in the gathering darkness, a huge heap of rocks, deposited here on the basin's floor by some ancient glacier and eroded by wind and rain into the semblance of a misshapen fortress.

She began whistling as she approached the rocks, a shrill tune that brought up the mare's ears; and then she paused to listen, and Johnny whistled from the shadows. She reined up and called his name softly. He emerged from the rock pile, leading his horse, and stood beside it, a slight figure in the gloom. He had about him an edginess of which Beth was immediately aware; and he said, his voice petulant, "I rode down last night. I expected you'd be along."

"I couldn't get away in the early evening. Not without Dad knowing and fretting. After that, I was busy. A stranger rode in with a wound Broken Box gave him."

Johnny was at once interested. "I heard them racketing around the range. I wondered what was up. Who was this stranger anyway?"

"A drifter." She busied herself at untying the grub sack, which she passed over to him. He hefted it, then transferred it to his own saddle horn.

"Tripp showed yet?" he asked.

She shook her head. "Corb thinks he never will."

Johnny grinned; there was just enough light for her to see that grin, and it was too much like Tripp's. "Because he dreamed the moon was made out of green cheese?"

"Johnny," she said with sudden earnestness, "why don't you ride out of here till all this blows over? Head down into Wyoming or over into Idaho. Get a job on some ranch, or just drift. Write me from wherever you are, and I'll let you know when the sign is clear to come back."

He stiffened. "Hugh McCoy's died. Is that it?"

"He was still alive—the last I heard."

Johnny's voice held a belligerent stubbornness. "I want to be around when the lid blows off."

"Why, Johnny? Why?"

"To side Tripp."

She had battered herself against this obstacle before, and she was tired of it. She thought: *Tripp! Always Tripp!* and felt defeated. She searched her mind for an argument that would touch the real goodness which she knew lay in Johnny, and she asked, "How many times do you think I'll ride over here with food before somebody spots me and follows?"

He frowned, but it was a thoughtful frown. "I don't like your doing this. I'll get by."

"On what, Johnny? It's too risky for you to come to Diamond L. You know that. You show yourself at some other ranch and how are you going to know whether that ranch hasn't decided to lean toward Broken Box? Once McCoy dies, the lines are bound to be drawn."

She could no longer see his expression; it had grown too dark; but his voice was somber. "I know, Beth. And I know how all this has been burdening you. Hell, Beth, *you're* Diamond L. Dad's drinking himself into a daze, and Corb's reading his damn' dream book and muttering to himself, and Tripp's so far away we can't be sure a letter gets to him. Me, I'm worse than useless. It's thinking about how things stand that makes me want to ride to Broken Box and call Luke Ramage out into the yard.

Beth said tonelessly, "The day you do that, we're all done for."

"I'm not so sure."

"Believe me, Johnny, you can't stop trouble by going out and starting it."

"Oh, hell!" Johnny said.

She had the feeling of having gone over this argument so many times that she could anticipate his every thought and word. He was so young, so very young; yet there was only two years between them. He walked in Tripp's shadow, not yet seeing that he must make his own. Still, this was her fight, to keep him from such folly; and she searched for words that would reach to him and be a hobble to his restive spirit, holding him back from Tripp's wild call.

And then suddenly he was up into saddle and leaning forward, his gun out in his hand and a taunt alertness in his voice. "Riders coming!" he said.

Johnny was only a vague form, and all else was lost in the starless dark; but she heard them, a couple of horsemen walking their mounts. She peered hard, but she couldn't be sure from which direction they approached and whether their trail would bring them closer. She whispered, "Broken Box!" and flicked at Johnny's horse with her quirt. "Ride, Johnny! Get out of here!"

"And leave you? I'll give them a fight first!"

Her quirt had barely touched Johnny's horse, but the mount reared. Johnny reined it to a stand. "Beth, hit for the rocks!"

Now a voice spoke out of the darkness, asking, "Who's there?"

Johnny tilted his gun with his free hand and fired, the gun making its red blossom and giving Beth a brief look at Johnny's hard-drawn face. Someone cursed in the shadows, and a gun spoke over there, the lead pinging against the rocks behind Johnny and Beth to ricochet away. The sound was high and thin and seemed to be searching.

Johnny shouted, "Come on up and fight, you sneaking sons!"

Beth again struck at his horse with her quirt, putting all the strength of her arm into the blow. The horse bolted forward so suddenly that her instant fear was that Johnny would be unseated. Then Johnny was gone into the night.

Beth swung her own horse about, and bending low over the horn, drove hard. Guns sounded behind her and about her, but she could only gallop blindly along, a sense of horrified unreality in her. She had matured in a violent land, and she had known guns all her years, but she had never been shot at before. Gun-play was something men talked about in the winter nights; gun-play was a legend attached in whispers to this man's name and that one's. Now she heard the whine of bullets and knew how deep-striking fear could be.

She rode until the horse began heaving beneath her, and then she reined short and sat listening. She found that her heart was pounding and her breath was a sob in her throat. She fought to quiet herself, then strained her ears. There was no sound of pursuit, but far off in the night she could hear the distant popping of shots; a man's shout was a fragment of sound. The Broken Box men who had clashed with them had taken Johnny's trail, and this brought her a second fear, greater than the one she'd know when the guns had been turned against her.

Johnny!

For a long while she sat her saddle, listening while the sound of guns grew more distant and finally dwindled away. Around her the night pressed, deep and forbidding. She had no choice but to find her way home, and this she did by making a wide arc that brought her to the ford. No man challenged her on that ride; no man awaited her at the river.

She attained the far bank and again sat listening, wondering about Johnny, wondering whether any man now lay dead on the other side of the Thief. The stars were out now, and they danced upon the placid face of the ford and mocked her.

Then she rode slowly back to Diamond L and came into the yard, where the dog greeted her. She got down from the horse and let the dog come close and identify her. She stood leaning against the horse, feeling done in, feeling defeated. Lamplight now sprang from the bunkhouse windows, and lamplight stood in the ranch-house, soft and warm. She put up her horse and walked to the gallery and mounted its steps, and she knew then that Corb Blount was inside with her father. Blount had fetched his Winchester as far as the gallery and left it standing just outside the door.

She looked at the rifle and shuddered; she had had more than enough of guns tonight. Again her thoughts turned to Clint Tracy and the reason she'd wanted him gone from here. That, too, was tied with guns. But suddenly she found herself wanting him back. She couldn't have explained this change in her. It did not cross her mind that she, too, needed a leaning post, now that the winds grew strong.

4. The Flickering Flame

RIDING NORTHWARD from Diamond L, Tracy came across a rolling land in the last of the daylight, the high distant hills marching to his left and his right and the basin an immense vagueness all around him, its contours mellowed by sunset. Night's coolness came down from the far slopes; and birds made small, hushed noises in the grass.

Tracy rode easily, favoring his wounded shoulder; and darkness came before his riding was done. He saw the lights of Spurlock from one of the rises, and other lights far flung in the vastness. He wondered if that was Broken Box over yonder, across the Thief, making its pin pricks toward the base of the eastern hills. He had no names for the other ranches.

This was mostly unfenced domain. Sometimes he came upon cattle and studied their brands, memorizing them. He was surprised that most of the cattle were native stock, with little of the longhorn strain showing. He was also surprised that the cattle were in fine shape, for Montana had come through a disastrous winter that had nearly wiped out cattledom. He finally concluded that this sheltered basin had been spared from the worst of the storms.

His thinking was idle, only something to while away the miles. He liked the being alone of this night riding; he was a man used to solitude and his own whimseys. He had been tethered to no man and no brand, not for long anyway. He had nearly denied Texas when Cappy Lovett had put the question to him a second time, yet Texas had been his origin. But that had been long ago. Texas was only the vague, scattered memories of an obscure boyhood. He had moved west with Texas's vast migration in search of new graze; and thus when he named any place home, it was Arizona. He had known no trade but that of horse and rope, and he had worked for one outfit and another in Arizona until the red chaos of the Graham-Tewksbury feud had come and caught him up and changed all his way of living. Now he was a man with a mission, and that seemed strange and burdensome. Always he had been footloose, and the old habits clung.

Thus it was that when he reached Spurlock, the notion came to him that he could just ride on.

It was the same temptation he had known at the Notch when he had first looked upon the basin, and he had thought that temptation had been conquered in Diamond L's yard. But tonight's riding had let him look at himself from afar, and the thing that had brought him to Montana now seemed involved and futile. He wondered if this would be his lot all the rest of his days, to wrestle with this troublesome decision; and he grew irritable with the thought, and stubborn. He stepped down from his saddle in Spurlock.

He saw the town as just another scatteration of clapboard and false fronts upon the prairie. He had seen enough like it in the long ride north, but there was this difference: Spurlock was the seat of Thief River Basin, and he had half-committed himself to the basin's affairs. Thus he gave the town his appraisal, memorizing it as he had memorized the brands. Spurlock squatted on the west bank of the Thief; a railroad spilled down from the far hills and ran through here, with shipping pens and loading chutes at

STRANGER FROM ARIZONA 33

the town's outskirts. These things Tracy noticed in his first sweeping glance.

After he'd tied up his horse, hunger sent him into a restaurant; and here he ate a solitary meal, taking his good time at it. On the wall of the booth, people had penciled their names while waiting to be served. He looked at these names, none having any meaning to him until he spied Tripp Lovett's. How long ago had it been written there? It struck him that Tripp Lovett was everywhere in this basin, in one form or another; and his food tasted like sand.

He could, by looking at a certain angle, see through the front window. Men came and went upon the street, cowmen, all. He thought of Diamond L and Broken Box and knew how it would be when the blowup came. All the others would be dragged in, having no more choice than the fat sheriff who was finding the fence too sharp to straddle.

Hap came into the restaurant and waddled to the counter and bought himself a cigar. He gnawed the end from it and clamped it between his teeth, but he didn't get around to lighting it. Someone said, "Howdy, Harriman"; and Tracy added the man's last name to his fund of knowledge. The sheriff spied Tracy and marked him as a stranger and gave him a sharp, measuring glance, saying nothing. The sheriff had a face grown shapeless with too much fat; he was a man troubled and morose.

Tracy finished his meal, dug out the makings and spun up a cigarette. Again he was mindful of his wounded shoulder. When a girl came to clear away the dishes, he asked, "Where will I find a doctor?"

The girl frowned. "There's only Smeed. I don't think he'd touch you right now. Not unless you were bad hurt and had to have him. He's got Hugh McCoy up in his quarters, too hurt to move, and McCoy's taking up all his time. The office is over the saddle shop."

Tracy went out to the street. Cottonwoods grew here, making a brave stand. Spurlock had a hotel, he saw, and a blacksmith shop and a mercantile and more than enough saloons. Most of the hitchrails were filled, but riders were still coming in. At this hour, the flung lamplight from doors and windows touched the dust stirred by their passage and made of it a golden haze that hung constantly in the air.

Finishing out his cigarette, Tracy put it under his heel, then walked along until he found the saddle shop. It was across the way, and above it a single window showed light. Tracy rested his shoulders against a wall and folded his arms and stood watching that light. He noticed that every man who passed along the street lifted his eyes to it.

One came by who was early drunk, an oldish man with a not-bright look to him. He regarded Tracy vaguely and said, "When the time comes for Smeed to pull the blanket over his face, he'll blow out the lamp. A man could start a betting pool on the minute and the hour, if he was so minded."

"Hell," Tracy said, not feeling callous but wanting to know how this townsman would react, "we've all got to die sometime."

The drunk shook his head. "When McCoy dies, everything dies."

Tracy moved on along the street. On the opposite side was a saloon with a sign naming it the Argonaut, and among the horses at its hitchrail he spied two bearing that angle brand he had first noticed on Herb's horse at the Notch. This he now knew was Broken Box, and at first it seemed strange to him that Broken Box men should be here liquoring with a roundup as yet unfinished. Then he judged that the riders had come to town to see how Hugh McCoy was doing.

While he stood watching, the boy Herb came out of the Argonaut and paused to take a slaunch-wise stand beneath the wooden awning, his pimpled face revealed by vagrant lamplight.

Tracy smiled, seeing the studied stance of Herb, the air of a man who had liquored with men and was now about other business. He had known a hundred Herbs, had Tracy;

but this one interested him in a queer way he couldn't have named. He saw Herb as an untrained colt who might be made tractable for the saddle or might go flinging his heels with the wild bunch. Yet the destinies of the Herbs were no concern of his, and he wondered why he wasted a thought on the boy. He saw Herb come down off the porch and lift himself to leather and ride out.

Tracy drew in a breath then, for Luke Ramage had appeared under the overhang.

Ramage stood there with a cigar in his teeth, looking big and formidable and self-satisfied, a square-faced man upon whom arrogance rested always, even in such a relaxed moment as this one. Tracy crossed over toward the man with no conscious prompting. He stopped at the foot of the steps below Ramage and said, "Evening," and waited to see what that would do to Ramage.

Broken Box's foreman almost answered in kind instinctively; then full recognition came into his eyes. His cigar sagged as his face fell apart with astonishment. Here was a man who'd thought another dead and learned his error.

Tracy pushed this moment as a fighter pushes a blow when his opponent is reeling. He said, "I'm with Diamond L now. I want you to know that. We'll be over to cut that herd one of these days."

Ramage had had his instant of uncertainty and surprise, but he got hold of himself fast. The hard truculence that had marked him at Broken Box's camp squared him up; and he said, "Do you think we'll let you?"

"And how can you stop us?" Tracy asked. "I saw how many strays you'd gather in."

"Stop you? Diamond L's an outlaw outfit, with Johnny Lovett hiding in the hills."

Tracy smiled. "Doc Smeed's light hasn't gone out yet."

"When it does," Ramage said, "we'll shoot any Diamond L man out of his saddle on sight."

The memory of last night with Broken Box hard on his heels grew strong in Tracy, and his temper rose and ruled him. He hunched his shoulders forward and let his arms hung slack. "Would you care to start the shooting now?" he demanded. "Or do you need deep dark, like last night, and all the odds stacked your way?"

Ramage colored, his own temper showing. But there was no fear in him; and that was the thing Tracy noted, wanting a complete judgment of the man.

Ramage said, "This makes twice you've braced me. Don't do it again." He moved down the steps past Tracy and climbed aboard his horse. Swinging the mount about, he walked it up the street, not looking back. Tracy watched him go and found his own hands trembling.

He cut his anger with whiskey inside the Argonaut, drinking alone. He was a stranger here and therefore got only the idle speculation of the others along the bar and the ones at the gaming tables. They hadn't heard what had passed between him and Ramage, so he was nothing to them as yet; he was a chip in nobody's game.

He fingered his empty glass and felt out the temper of this place, and it came to him that a dark mood held here, with nothing of normal revelry in it. This same mood was upon all Spurlock, now that he thought back to restaurant and street. That was what had brought him here, his wanting to know how Spurlock stood. The town was waiting out the last tag end of waiting.

He looked at himself in the bar mirror, seeing a face that had attracted both men and women, a strong face turned the color of saddle leather by Arizona's suns. He had bleached-out eyebrows and a cleft chin, and he guessed he liked his face as well as the next. He remembered Broken Box's talk of him last night. "Old eyes in a young face," Ramage had said. "A loose way of handling himself like maybe he was afraid of a tap on the shoulder..." He thought of Beth Lovett then and wondered again about his mission, wondered if a man could ever ride away from his yesterdays.

Harriman came into the saloon and bent his gaze about until he sighted Tracy. He moved over and stood at Tracy's elbow and held silent for so long that Tracy finally asked, "What's bothering you?"

Harriman cleared his throat. "That your sorrel tied up in front of Sally's restaurant?"

Not turning, Tracy looked at the sheriff in the bar mirror and nodded.

"Don't recollect ever seeing the brand before."

"It came from a long way off," Tracy said. "Maybe as far away as the other side of the hills. It might even be from outside your county, sheriff."

"Drifting?"

"Maybe."

"A drifting gun, I'm thinking, smelling out trouble and hoping to hire out somewheres. You'd better drift on."

"Sheriff," Tracy asked, "did Luke Ramage stop and have a word with you before he cleared town?"

Harriman colored slightly and covered his confusion with a blustery tone. "Suppose he did!"

"I wondered," Tracy said. "Do you always take orders from him?"

Harriman said, "Don't push me, stranger. I eat out of no man's hand. Anybody will tell you that."

"Look," Tracy said patiently, "you saw my horse in Diamond L's corral this afternoon and read its brand. But you didn't come looking for me till you talked with Ramage. Now what side of the fence does that put you on?"

Harriman swallowed hard. "None, mister. Just keep clear of trouble if you stay around."

"Sure," said Tracy.

Still not turning, he watched the sheriff's reflection as Harriman waddled out. Ordering a second drink, Tracy stood toying with it. And then suddenly there was another chore to be done, and with the realization he wondered if this new idea hadn't been in a corner of his mind ever since he'd decided to come to town.

He put his glass down and strode out of the saloon and turned toward the saddle shop. But as he came abreast of a shadowy slot between two of the buildings, a voice called to him softly. "Tracy! Clint Tracy!"

He knew that voice. And because he did, he came to a stop with a wild sense of unreality, a feeling that he had not crossed Utah's miles and Wyoming's at all but was now awakening back in Arizona to find the long trail a dream.

The man who stood waiting was a tall angular shape with a dark, saturnine face that had a perpetual grin. Tracy knew that his own astonishment must be naked on his face; and he said with no affability, "Howdy, Ringo."

Ringo said easily, "You don't have to be edgy, *amigo*. Arizona is over and done with. I drew my pay and did my work. So did you. If you can't smell sheep on me, I can't smell cow on you. I'd buy a drink, but maybe we'd better make medicine first."

Tracy said, "Montana is a long way from where the trail started. I passed through a lot of towns. It couldn't be just *luck* that landed us both in the same one."

Ringo's grin kept his lean face ajar. Always he had this high good humor on him; but Tracy knew the shallowness of it, for Ringo was a man born cornered and knowing only how to claw his way out. "Tripp told me about the trouble up here," Ringo said. "It didn't interest Tripp—not when it meant fighting for free. With you and me it could be different. Mebbeso you got wind of that?"

Tracy asked, "Have you bought in yet?"

Ringo shook his head. "The bidding will be higher when they get a real fight going."

"And your gun is for the highest bidder?"

Ringo shrugged. "We could do business as a team, Tracy. Two gun-hands who cut their teeth at Pleasant Valley, all wrapped up as one package."

Tracy took a step toward him and said through his teeth, "This is the way it will be, and I want you to get it straight: We've met before, so we speak when we come face to face. But I don't know anything about you, and you know less about me. Do you savvy? Outside of that, you walk wide of me, Ringo. Because if you don't, I'm going to kill you!"

Ringo's grin stayed, but now it had teeth in it. "Pleasant Valley is a finished fight. You got no call to be arching your back at me now, Tracy."

"My reasons are my own, Ringo. Just remember what I've said."

Ringo's eyes took on a hard, savage shine. "You've called the dance, Tracy, and named the tune. Walk wide of me too. I've tried to put out a paw to you, and you've slapped it down. The hell with you!"

Tracy said again, "Just remember," and turned and walked on.

He paused after a few paces and built up another cigarette and took three drags from it and flung it aside. He thought: *Ringo!* and was still astonished, even though he knew how Ringo came to be here. He thought then: *Ringo knows!* and he wondered what Ringo would do with his knowledge. Tracy knew the man, so the answer was painfully simple. Everything that Ringo had was for sale.

He almost turned back to seek out Ringo, to make some real compromise with him or to force a finish fight if need be. And while he waited, struggling with himself, a small, stoop-shouldered man came out of the door of the covered stairway clinging to the side of the saddle shop and crossed obliquely toward the restaurant. The man wore a shabby black suit and had a preoccupied air, and Tracy judged him to be Doc Smeed stealing time from his patient for a quick supper. He was reminded then of what his intention had been when Ringo had accosted him. He had had his excuse to see Smeed—there was his wounded shoulder—but now the opportunity he'd wanted was even better, with Smeed gone from his quarters. So Tracy hurried on and climbed the darkness of the stairway and put his hand to Doc Smeed's door.

He found himself in a dim office with a roll-top pigeonhole desk, a swivel chair, a dusty bookcase, and a small pot-bellied stove. The smell of medicine was here, and the smell of sickness. Beyond the outer office, dim lamplight shone through an open doorway; and in there was a bed, one end visible from where Tracy stood. Tracy stepped through the doorway and looked at the man in the bed. Hugh McCoy lay ashen-faced and unconscious, a big man, a grizzled man, a stout oak cut down.

He had hoped to read McCoy, had Tracy; but there was no reading him, for this was the shadow of the man rather than the substance. Arrogant? That lined, leathery face might have borne such a stamp, but pain had erased it. The jaw was a fighter's but the eyes were closed. And it was always the eyes that made a window by which you looked into a man.

Tracy stepped nearer the bed and stood gazing directly down; and in that hushed moment, McCoy opened his eyes and said vaguely, "What time is it, Luke?"

"It's evening, Hugh," Tracy said softly. "You've been sick."

"Time enough to ride to town?" McCoy asked in that same mindless voice.

"Time enough for everything," Tracy said, but he knew it was a lie.

The mist cleared from McCoy's eyes, and he gave Tracy a sharp, aggressive look. "Who the hell are you?"

Yes, arrogance was there and something else besides, a stubborn sort of courage.

Tracy said, "Take it easy. You've been having a bad time of it."

McCoy looked about him, a sort of wildness in his eyes. It seemed to Tracy that he could see the man's thought slowly moving to fill the empty vistas of such an awakening. McCoy tried raising himself; the effort was too much for him. "Doc Smeed's?" he asked.

Tracy nodded. "You were shot—bushwhacked. Do you remember?"

McCoy said, "Ah, yes." His eyes measured Tracy and weighed him and probed him, cutting deep. McCoy's speech became precise, terribly precise. "Will . . . you . . . go . . . get . . . Hap . . . Harriman?"

"Whatever you want to tell Harriman, you'd better tell me," Tracy said.

A spasm crossed McCoy's face, and his eyes closed again. The life went out of his face, leaving only the ashen pallor; and he seemed not to be breathing. Tracy bent close to the man, a desperation in him, a desire to reach out and hold life in McCoy by the power of his hands. "What is it you want to tell Harriman? McCoy! Speak up!"

Without opening his eyes, McCoy made the attempt, but his mind had shifted to another man. "Tell Luke—" he said. "Tell Luke—" He sighed then; the sigh became a shudder, and that was the end of it.

Tracy straightened up, his frustration a hard, tight core in his belly. He had seen the man die; and with McCoy had died everything, just as the drunk had prophesied. He had known his temptation, had Tracy; but now he saw himself committed irrevocably to Diamond L, for if McCoy had lived, there might have been no fight and no need for a drifter to buy in. Now the choice was really made.

Tracy glanced toward the lamp that burned on a table beside the window. The time had come to blow out the light. Without meaning to, he crossed toward the lamp and then remembered himself.

He looked through the window, standing back from it so as not to show; he looked upon the main street of Spurlock. Across the way, at almost the precise spot where Tracy had stood earlier in the evening, a high, angular form leaned against a building. All Spurlock had watched the window, waiting for a light to die and the man to die and the last hope of peace in Thief River Basin to die, too. And Ringo was now another who waited along with the rest of them.

5. War Talk

HE WITHDREW from the window with a feeling of being trapped, not by the waiting Ringo but by a web of circumstances that had had its beginning in Arizona. Now it had been given to him to see Hugh McCoy die, and that, too, had been destiny's doing. Five minutes more in the Argonaut—five minutes more at his meeting with Ringo—and he might have found only a corpse here. Still, he had learned almost nothing from McCoy. And so he stood indecisively, not quite sure what his next move should be, knowing only that he must get out of here.

Crossing the room, Tracy had a last look at the dead man and a quick glance around to make certain he'd left no sign of his own presence. Also, he looked for a second door giving from this place, but there was none. He came through Smeed's office and down the covered stairway to linger just within its dark maw and have another look across the street. Ringo was still there, tall and thin and saturnine, a black vulture waiting for death. He was merely idle, from the look of him. Because Tracy knew him also to be restless, he gambled that Ringo would soon move along.

And so Tracy waited, his palms growing sticky and his skin itching with the waiting. Suppose Ringo had seen him turn into the stairway! Probably Ringo would continue waiting then, knowing that Tracy would sooner or later have to show himself.

Tracy wanted no man to remember afterwards that he had been with Hugh McCoy at the death, for tonight he had named himself a Diamond L man, and Ramage would certainly tie one fact to the other. Now Tracy fretted lest Doc Smeed return and find him loitering in the stairway and draw a true surmise later. Tracy had lost all sense of time in those last minutes while McCoy's life had flickered out; he could make only a poor guess as to when Smeed would come back. Soon, he supposed. He stared at Ringo and in his mind willed Ringo to be on his way. And at last Ringo built up a cigarette, fired it, and moved along the street.

Whereupon Tracy crossed quickly to his horse, lifted himself to the saddle, and jerked at the tie-rope. He had a look along Spurlock's false-fronts. The town seemed peaceful; the town still waited. He glanced through the restaurant's window, thinking he might catch a glimpse of Smeed. Then he lined out southward for Diamond L.

He rode hard and straight, holding the horse to a steady, mile-eating gallop as long as he could, then walking the mount whenever it began to flag. Always, though, the cry in Tracy was to hurry. He now had some familiarity with the terrain, and he made use of this, skirting the rises whenever he could and finding the easiest traveling. In his mind he could still see McCoy lying dead. He had gained a knowledge a few minutes before all of Spurlock would have gained it, and he was carrying that knowledge to Diamond L. He had no other plan—not at first. The plan came later, somewhere in that wild ride.

The stars told him midnight was near when he sighted Lovett's spread; but light still showed in the ranch-house, just as it had showed at a late hour last night. He judged then that Diamond L had long waited, too, even as Spurlock had waited.

The dog greeted him noisily, and the ranch-house door sprang open again. A yellow rectangle of light lay upon the hard-packed yard, and a figure moved in this light. Tracy put his horse in the corral as Beth came toward him. He came out of the corral and faced her. Some of the grim urgency of the ride still clung to Tracy, making his words brusquer than he meant them to be. He said, "McCoy's dead."

She stood stock still, her face a pale outline. Then she made some wavering motion with her hands like a blind person reaching for support. "No!" she said. "It can't be. It mustn't be."

Tracy said relentlessly, "Where's Johnny hiding, girl? How soon can we fetch him in?"

Her eyes touched him and were full of attention. His question might have been a peg which she grasped. "You want Johnny to turn himself in? Is that it?"

He put his hands on her shoulders. "You know where Johnny is. You must know. If he'd trust anybody on this ranch, he'd trust you. Can't you see there's only one thing to do?"

He had not seen her surety so shaken before. She might have been a small girl lost in the vastness of a world of harsh realities. Her face puckered, and she looked as though she were going to cry. She said numbly, "It's too important a thing for me to decide alone."

"Then let's talk to your dad. Is he up?"

She nodded.

"We can't waste time," he said.

She led the way to the house; and he followed her to the parlor where the ceiling light burned dimly and Cappy Lovett sat deep in the green plush chair, an old man lost in his dreaming. Corb Blount was here, too, a morose, silent heap of a man, giving the room a grayness by his presence. They were a pair at once together and apart; they sat within these walls with no camaraderie between them.

Beth looked at them both and spared them no more than Tracy had spared her. "Hugh McCoy has died," she said.

Lovett seemed almost asleep. His hands lay idle in his lap, and at first he did not stir. He was this way for a long moment; the lamp spluttered in the silence, and then Lovett sighed. "Old Hugh.... This hits me mighty hard. We were good friends once."

Pity touched Tracy, and the words became an echo in his mind, fashioning pictures. "Good friends..." Two men coming up out of Texas in Reconstruction days, hazing their herds before them the breadth of the nation to this basin and being neighbors in that first loneliness. Two men fighting Indians and then rustlers. Two men made akin by background and by adversity, holding steadfast, holding to friendship until one had grown so big as to crowd the other's graze and the cord of friendship had been stretched to the breaking point.

Probably there had been some little thing at first—some small beginning to a long chain of incidents. A stray on another man's graze... a fence cut out of necessity and left unmended... a puncher from one crew elbowing a puncher from the other at a bar... harsh words and quick tempers. And then the war clouds had gathered and stood black over the basin.

And now Hugh McCoy lay dead.

Blount raised his eyes and said to no one, "McCoy asked for it. That is why I can feel no real regret. He sowed the wind and reaped the whirlwind."

His was an unimaginative man's practical judgment, given without rancor, given without charity. Here was a man who had never let sentiment slow his hand or soften his blow, one whose thinking was unleavened by any need but the need of his brand. Sensing this, Tracy saw him as an ally of the moment and therefore spoke to him. "Johnny's got to turn himself in."

Beth said, "I don't know. In Harriman's jail, he'd be where Broken Box could find him."

Tracy turned to her. "Tonight Harriman told me he ate out of no man's hand. Can we count on that?"

Blount frowned. "It is my thought that Harriman has

never been put to a test. But in my opinion a prisoner would be safe with him. Still, what do we gain if Johnny takes the risk?"

Tracy spread his hands. "I babbled about the Graham-Tewksbury trouble last night. Before Arizona, they'd been friends in Texas, too. The Tewksburys brought sheep into the Tonto Basin; the Grahams defended cattle graze. There was big trouble—hangings and bushwhackings and back-shootings. Before it was over, twenty-six cattlemen and six sheepmen were dead."

Blount asked, "How does that concern us?"

"Do you want that kind of war along Thief River? I talked to Luke Ramage tonight. If Johnny turns outlaw, then all Diamond L is outlaw. Let a range war really start, and every other ranch in the basin will be drawn in on one side or the other. Man, I've seen what that can mean. I don't want to see it again."

Blount's puritanical face became furrowed with thought. He worked at his thinking; and Tracy began to fret. Time was a broken bottle with its contents spilling out beyond reclaim. Couldn't Blount see that?

But Blount's face was cold and uncompromising. "Broken Box has got Diamond L cattle in its gather," he said. "Maybe some of our critters crossed at the ford, or maybe Ramage's roundup took in both sides of the Thief. We let McCoy graze this bank a few seasons back. That was our first mistake." He glanced at Cappy Lovett. "You'll mind I told you so at the time." He looked again at Tracy. "And that is why I say our first job should be to take what is ours. I am for cutting Broken Box's herd."

Tracy said patiently, "I've heard talk in this house of a Winchester cut. Do that and ordinarily you'd have the sympathy of every man in the basin. The difference now is that Hugh McCoy is dead and Johnny Lovett is hiding. There'll be time to haze Diamond L cattle out of Broken Box's herd once we've mended our own fence."

"Right is right," Blount said stubbornly. "They are our cattle."

"How many men have you got in your bunkhouse?"

"Six."

"A lot more than that ride for Broken Box," Tracy said. "I know; I had a chance to count 'em. *Might* is right as long as people think Hugh McCoy's blood is on this doorstep." He looked at Beth. "I heard what you told Harriman this afternoon. I couldn't help hearing it. The only thing against Johnny is that he cut and ran. And the best way for us to confound Ramage is for Johnny to knock on Harriman's door and say he's willing to stand trial."

She stood there indecisive, her face tortured, her eyes dark with worry. She made a mute appeal to her father, a quick gesture of her hands.

Lovett said in his gentle voice, "Tripp will be home any day now. He'll know what to do about this. Johnny will come out of hiding if Tripp tells him to. Johnny sets a great store by Tripp. You recollect how Johnny followed him around when he was a button? Now Tripp—"

"Dad," Beth said firmly, "Tripp isn't here."

"But he's on his way. I wouldn't be surprised to hear him out there in the yard any minute now."

"Look," Tracy interjected. "What ways can a man get into this basin except by rail into Spurlock or over the Notch by saddle horse?"

Lovett showed surprise. "None. Unless he wants to pick a trail across the hills."

"Then you're wasting your time with that telescope. Broken Box has got gun guards at the Notch. Maybe they're waiting for Tripp Lovett. Maybe they're making sure Johnny doesn't leave. More likely they're set to stop any man who might drift in and be hired by Diamond L. I should know. They stopped me yesterday. And they got jumpy when I noticed too many Diamond L cows around. That's how I ended up on your doorstep with a bullet hole in me. You might as well quit counting on Tripp Lovett."

The old man took on the stricken look of one who has found the ground cut from under him. He was lost and alone, his hands making feeble, fluttering motions, but only for a moment. His hope was a banner that unfurled to any breeze. "I didn't know they were guarding the Notch," he said. "But Tripp will find a way to fool them. He's mighty smart, that boy." He looked at Blount. "They'll have to get up early to beat Tripp, won't they, Corb?"

"Tripp!" Beth said with great exasperation.

Lovett said, "He's just the boy to ride through those gun guards like they were a paper wall."

"Oh, hell!" Tracy said and knew that no logic could be pitted against this blind worship of Cappy Lovett's. Therefore he made his appeal to the other two, flinging it out with a tone of finality. "Do we ride after Johnny?"

Blount shrugged. "It's not for me to say. I don't even know where he is hiding."

"I do," Beth Lovett said.

Her father said in a preoccupied manner, "You do whatever you think best, girl."

Blount said, "Just a minute." He got up and moved behind his chair and put his hands on the back of it. His knuckles showed white; his face was a mask in the lamplight. "There is one question I must ask. What is your stake in this matter, Mr. Tracy?"

Tracy said, an edge to his voice, "When your house is on fire, do you ask questions of the man who wants to throw a bucket of water on it?"

Blount stood inflexible. "You brushed with Broken Box," he said. "You stumbled in here afterwards. You heard talk enough to know that we are against Broken Box. Are we the handle by which you are going to lift your own troubles?"

"If I wanted to make trouble, I'd be backing your notion of cutting Broken Box's herd at once," Tracy snapped. He spread his hands again, seeking words that might allay the suspicion of this blunt, morose man, yet have the ring of logic to them. He said, "Maybe I've seen one Tonto Basin war too many. I've told you about that. I don't want

Johnny Lovett thrown to the wolves. But better that than thirty dead men."

Beth said, "You're right. I'll take you to him. He's at Orlando."

The name meant nothing to Tracy. His only feeling was one of triumph and relief. He had won her over, and in his mind he quickly backtrailed through all this talk, seeking the point where he had convinced her of the sense of his plan. She was a brave girl and shrewd, and he supposed she was thinking of whatever was best for Diamond L in the long run. Yet it wasn't quite as pat as that. Somewhere he had touched a hidden need in her, a hidden fear that had made the difference.

Suddenly he was struck by the change in her since he had ridden away from Diamond L; and he guessed then that something had happened during those few hours. The news of Hugh McCoy's passing could not alone account for the sickness in her eyes. But there was no time now for probing, so he only asked, "Orlando? Is it a long ride?"

"Orlando is a ghost town up in the hills, all that's left of a gold strike of the sixties. We could make it there before daylight."

Cappy Lovett looked surprised. "Orlando? Now who'd have thought of that?" He began to smile. "That's one on Broken Box! Damned if it isn't. It's the kind of trick Tripp would have pulled."

Tracy was mortally tired in spite of his sleep during the day. His wound had taken that much toll of him—the wound and all the tensions of Spurlock and the wild ride afterwards and his pitting himself against these people. Yet he said, "Will you lead the way?"

She had her last instant of hesitation; it passed as a shadow passes, and she nodded.

But Blount said, "I must warn you, Elizabeth. I have never found any way of dealing with rogues but the direct way. The grass belongs to the gun-swift, and our trail should be leading us across the river. This is no time for deviousness, and no time for trusting strangers. Why has this man taken it upon himself to learn so much about us in so short a time? Have you thought of that?"

"Come," Beth said and beckoned to Tracy.

Blount's voice was like a flung spear in the room. "If you are for Diamond L, you will find me a strong friend, Mr. Tracy. If this scheme of yours proves otherwise and harm comes to either of the children, I shall kill you."

Tracy said, "I'm tired of you, Blount. I'm as tired of you as one man can get of another. So far there has been nothing from you but talk."

"Don't be deceived," Blount said.

Beth had already turned toward the door, and Tracy followed her. Blount's impersonal animosity seemed to be hard at his heels, making a heaviness in the air. Outside the door, he saw the Winchester leaning. He looked at the rifle and felt that he was looking at Blount. He crossed to the corral with Beth, and at her invitation he cut out a fresh Diamond L horse for himself. He saddled for both of them; and when they were mounted, he neck-reined across the yard, facing west toward the hills, stark and distant in the night.

"This way," Beth said, beckoning to him again.

"East?" he asked, astonished.

"Yes," she said. "Orlando is over there."

He squinted hard, wondering if he'd got his geography mixed. "And so is Broken Box, if I've got the lay of the land."

"Orlando was Johnny's choice," she said. "He reasoned that outside of Hap Harriman, only Ramage's crew would be interested in cutting sign of him. If you were Broken Box, would you expect to find Johnny Lovett on the *east* side of Thief River? You see, he fooled them by hiding in their own back yard."

Tracy whistled softly, knowing now why Cappy Lovett had been surprised when Orlando was named and pleased because Johnny had shown Tripp's own kind of daring.

Tracy thought of Luke Ramage then and how it would hit Ramage if the man could know where his quarry lurked. In his mind he pictured Ramage's chagrin, and he threw back his head and laughed.

6. Long Stirrup, Sharp Spur

LUKE RAMAGE had tarried in Spurlock for a word with Hap Harriman; and then the Broken Box foreman struck south from the town, big and blocky in the saddle, an angry man who reined his temper as he reined his horse, using a hard hand. He had long been driven by a bitter ambition; but always he was a careful schemer who guarded against his own explosiveness, knowing that rage sullied his judgment and weakened his wariness. But tonight he had gotten a jolting surprise when he'd encountered that stranger from Arizona before the Argonaut; and he was too proud a man to have liked the challenge the drifter had made—the challenge he had refused to accept.

"Would you care to start the shooting now?" the man had asked. The words still rang in Luke Ramage's ears.

It had not been fear, though, that had stayed his hand. He was, as Tracy had first judged him to be, a man who rode with a long stirrup and a sharp spur, a hard-driving man, but above all, one who believed there was a time and a place for everything. He preferred to choose both so that they gave him an edge; and in that respect also Tracy's judgment had been correct. Yet Ramage's backing down had given the drifter half a victory, and this thought rankled Ramage now. His greater anger came from the sorry knowledge that the man was alive when he had believed him dead.

"Damn him!" Ramage said aloud to the night.

At the ford, he splashed across the silent Thief; and as he veered south again, he hunched forward, peering ahead for sight of Herb. The kid had had very little start from town on Ramage; but Herb liked to gallop, fancying any ride as some sort of race. Ramage had long ago learned that the slow man often got there first; he had learned patience in a rough school. Many times he'd had to warn Herb about the way he handled horseflesh, and sometimes he'd threatened to fire him.

Tonight he wondered why he'd kept the boy. Herb had drifted in a year or so before, looking as shaggy as a wolf whelp and about as vicious. Ramage had hired him against Hugh McCoy's better judgment. Ramage had seen Herb as clay that might be molded to his own use, for even then he'd foreseen a day when he would want a hard crew.

Just now he had a few words to say to Herb, but he made no real effort to overtake the boy. *The hell with him!* Yet Ramage's anger was that much sharper when he rode into Broken Box's ranchyard.

Hugh McCoy had built on the basin's flat floor, midway between the Thief and the eastern hills, wanting his headquarters between winter and summer graze. His place sprawled without pattern, a scatteration of log buildings centered by a huge ranch-house, formidable as the man who'd reared it and somehow expressing his own rugged personality.

Ramage liked that house. He was an underling within its walls, but now he rode past it and looked upon the dwelling with new eyes, at last fancying himself its master. This dream had been denied him until tonight. He thought: *By grab, I'll eat at his table and sleep in his bed from here on out.* He liked that thought.

Coming to the corral, he put his horse away, noticing at once that Herb's mount wasn't within the peeled-pole enclosure. Then he gravitated toward the blacksmith shop, where metal rang against metal, clamorous in the night, and red fire showed, and the yellow eye of a lantern.

The chuck wagon had been fetched north from the roundup camp late that afternoon, for the cook had made profane complaint about a loose tire on one of the wheels. When Ramage came to the blacksmith shop doorway, he found Cultus and one of the younger hands at work beside the forge. Ramage watched them in silence as Cultus gave the wheel a last blow with the sledge, then signaled his helper, who hoisted the water bucket and sloshed water around the rim, cooling the metal and shrinking it into place.

When the sizzling had ceased, Ramage asked, "Where's Herb?"

Cultus inclined his head southward. "Rode through a short spell back. Went on to the camp."

Ramage frowned. "George," he told Cultus' helper, "you drive the chuck wagon back down there and tell Herb I want to see him. Tonight!"

George said, "Sure."

"Come along," Ramage said to Cultus and turned and strode toward the ranch-house, his boots beating heavily against the hard-packed yard.

The main room of the house was a cavernous place, with a stone fireplace filling one end, and smoke blackened rafters looming above. The furnishings had been hand-fashioned with a view to utility. No woman had graced Broken Box's house, not ever; and no kindly portraits smiled from the walls, no calico showed at the windows, no color softened the drabness of wood and stone and rawhide. The only rugs were bear skins, tokens of Hugh McCoy's prowess with a rifle. Into this room Luke Ramage strode, and at his heels came Cultus. Ramage got a lamp burning and dropped his hat on the handiest table.

"The air's got a bite to it these nights," he said. "Build a fire."

Cultus went about the task silently. He was a grizzled man, saddle warped and leathery, the oldest of Broken Box's crew both in years and service. He had come from Texas with Hugh McCoy and known the basin before a house had stood here. He got a small blaze going in the fireplace and stood with his back to it, looking at Ramage in a mild manner, waiting for whatever word Ramage had brought from town.

Ramage saw the unasked question on Cultus' face and was deliberately slow with the answer. To this extent his black mood had mastered him; but at last he said, "He was still alive when I left."

Cultus said, "Hugh's whang leather. He'll take a heap of killing."

Ramage dropped into a chair and shook his massive head. "I talked to Smeed. The doc figures that Hugh will go before the night's over. He's given up hope, Smeed has. There's just a chance, though, that Hugh will come awake before the end. Sometimes they do."

"Awake long enough to name Johnny Lovett?"

The question brought a quick, hard shine to Ramage's eyes. "What difference does that make? Johnny did the job, sure as hell."

Cultus looked down at his hands. Ropes had scarred them, and the years had made his knuckles stiff and knobby. "I'd want to make mighty sure," he said. "Hugh was my friend, Luke. So was Cappy Lovett. Once."

"Hugh will be dead when the sun comes up," Ramage said bluntly. "That's all we've got to think about. The question is: what happens when he's dead?"

"He's got no kin,' Cultus said slowly. "I'm certain sure of that. I don't know just how the law works in a case like this. Maybe there's a will. But if I know Hugh, there ain't. He wasn't figgerin' on dying. Not yet a spell."

"Then the ranch is sure as hell ours," Ramage said. He leaned back in the chair and half closed his eyes, looking at Cultus from under the lids, watching to see how Cultus took this.

Cultus shook his head. "I don't see how you can figger that way."

"Man, the ranch will belong to whoever holds it. That'll be us. And we'll spread it to both sides of the river, once we knock out Diamond L. Why not? Do you reckon Hap Harriman is going to ride out here with legal papers and toss 'em into our teeth? Hap wouldn't give an argument to anybody who showed him force."

Again he watched Cultus closely, and he saw a doubting look come over the old man's leathery face. It was not opposition but rather a lack of surety; yet it irritated Ramage, and he felt the tug of temper. "Well, what's eating at you?" he demanded. "You afraid of Harriman?"

Cultus said, "This ain't the smoky seventies. We're about ten years too late, Luke, for that kind of play. You're figgerin' on the weakness of Harriman the man. It's what Harriman stands for that's going to be mighty big to buck. Me, I'm a little old to turn owlhooter. I'd rather cut loose and drift."

Ramage said tonelessly, "You fool! There'll never be another chance like this in your lifetime or mine!"

Cultus said, "I've watched you. I've seen the way you've looked at this house and these acres. I can understand a man's cravin' them, but not as bad as you do."

Ramage said, "And you're wondering why. Is that it?"

Cultus nodded.

Ramage closed his eyes, every line of his face turning rigid. "I grew up along the Union Pacific right of way," he said. "I knew every dirty, rotten tent town from Julesburg to Promontory Point. I never rightly knew who my father and mother was; Ramage was the name of a gambler who raised me. I shilled for him. We moved from camp to camp as the rails moved; and I got kicks and cuffs for my pay. When I was sixteen, the year they drove the golden spike, I was bigger than that two-bit tinhorn. I jumped him one night and used my fists and boots on him, and maybe I left him dead. I never went back to see. That was at Laramie. Later I drifted from cowcamp to cowcamp—Wyoming, Utah, Nevada, Idaho, and then Montana. I've seen 'em all. I learned a little savvy along the way, enough to make myself foreman here. I've been on this spread ten years, Cultus. Longer than I ever stayed anywhere else. I'm not leaving it."

"Hell," Cultus said, his face showing an old man's envy, "you've got all the years ahead."

Ramage opened his eyes. "All my life I've wanted a chunk of ground I could call my own. When I saw this one, I knew this was it. I've got as much right to it as any man. More, in fact. I sweated harder than Hugh McCoy these last few years to make it what it is. Winter and summer. I liked Hugh, Cultus, as much as I've ever let myself like any man. But he's just so much bear meat the minute he dies. I can hold this ranch if I've got you and the crew to help me. I can build it into the biggest spread in this part of Montana. I've told you more about myself tonight than I've told any other man. I want you to savvy that hell or high water won't budge me. Will you string along?"

Cultus shrugged. "Where would I drift to?"

"Ah," Ramage said, "Now you're showing sense!"

Cultus said shrewdly, "The way I swing is the way the crew will swing. You know that, I reckon."

Ramage said, "I'll take care of all of you. You can tell the boys that."

Cultus held silent for a long moment. A stick exploded in the fireplace; a winged creature batted at the lamp. "I've got a strong stomach," Cultus said then, "but not as strong as yours. If I've got to line sights on Johnny Lovett, I've got to be sure he's the man."

Ramage looked sharply at Cultus and made an accurate guess. "Twice now you've mentioned Johnny. Something happened tonight, eh?"

"Early in the evening. Just after dark came down.

Sherm and Fletch rode back from town. They ran into Johnny up by that big rock heap east of the ford. Somebody was with Johnny. His sister, they think. Johnny fired at them; they shot back and gave him a chase. He got away."

"Johnny on *this* side of the Thief?" Ramage asked in amazement. He frowned, trying to make out the whys and wherefores of such a piece of news.

Cultus nodded. "This side, Luke."

Ramage said thoughtfully, "We'll find out about that. Pronto." He frowned again. "If I'm boss, you're the foreman now. We've got to keep the crew from scattering around. I haven't been pushing the roundup hard, not with so much trouble in the wind. But half the boys were in town tonight. Sherm and Fletch and Herb all left before I did, and I saw a few horses at the hitchrails as I rode out. Corb Blount's the joker in the deck, Cultus. If he comes over here with blood in his eye and a rifle across his saddle, looking for Diamond L cattle, I want somebody around."

Cultus cocked his head. "I think Herb just rode into the yard."

Ramage heard it, too, the thunder of hoofs as a rider roared recklessly up to the house. Herb's boots hit the gallery steps. He flung himself through the doorway and stood in the room, young and sure of himself. He said, "George caught up with me on the way to camp, Luke. He said you wanted me in a hurry. I rode hard."

Ramage said sourly, "There was no need to go killing the horse."

"Hell," said Herb, "what's a horse for but to ride?"

All his anger of the miles from Spurlock came back to Ramage then and focused on Herb. He had the key to this boy, had Ramage: Herb fancied himself tough, but he had always walked wide of Ramage, knowing the foreman to be tougher. And now Ramage said softly, "Come over here, Herb."

"Sure," said Herb and crossed the room to where Ra-

STRANGER FROM ARIZONA 59

mage sat. There was a swagger to Herb's walk. Ramage looked up at him, seeing the cocksure set to that slack mouth, the arrogance that had grown in Herb this past twenty-four hours. Big across the britches, this boy. At least in his own mind.

Ramage said, "I've been meaning to have a talk with you ever since last night, kid. That was a nice piece of work you did."

"Like shooting a sitting duck," said Herb. "There he was in the river, as open a target as you'd want. Maybe I was careless when I brought him down from the Notch. But I sure as hell made up for that when we took out after him."

"You rode hard, Herb," Ramage said. "And you shot straight. You're a ringtailed rannyhan in a tight, no doubt about it. But it was a mite dark. You sure you got him?"

"I saw him go into the river."

Now Ramage was done at playing cat-and-mouse, and he smiled sourly. "Then maybe you'd like to know that he braced me in Spurlock tonight. In front of the Argonaut. Walked up and told me he's working for Diamond L now. Not ten minutes after you'd left the bar!"

Herb's shoulders slumped as though the bones had been plucked from them, and his mouth twisted open. He stood stunned, seeing his glory turn to a ghost, fast fading. Defiance braced him for a single moment, some last shred of the boldness that had been his today; and he shouted, "You're crazy! I saw him go into the river!"

Ramage launched himself out of the chair and took a lunging step toward Herb. He slapped the boy, an openhanded blow that left his fingermarks on Herb's pasty face. Herb's hands came up instinctively, but Ramage batted them down, still keeping his own hands open. Ramage said, red rage in his voice, "Get back to the roundup camp! And stay there until you have different orders. Next time you bring a report that a man is dead, be mighty sure he *is* dead. Now get the hell out of my sight!"

Herb stared at him, sick with humiliation, then slowly

raised his hand to his cheek. Ramage half raised his own hand again, and Herb backed away. Hate was in the youngster's eyes—a killing hate—but his fear was greater. This Ramage knew, and he kept his face relentless. Herb turned toward the door and ran through it. Soon the beat of his horse's hoofs rose again out of the night.

Cultus said mildly, "You were a mite rough on him, Luke. I'd watch my back from here on out, was I you."

Ramage still stood, his eyes hot. "I took his word last night. I walked right into that drifter tonight. It wouldn't have happened if that kid had told it straight."

Cultus shrugged and bent down to feed the fire. He didn't speak until he had finished and stood up again. "What's one stray rider more or less? Last night we went foggin' it around like all hell depended on nailing him. Looking back, it seems a little loco. We can't make every saddle bum go to work for Broken Box."

Ramage turned to him. "He came looking for Cappy Lovett. Do you remember that? Cultus, that fellow worried me from the first time I laid eyes on him, and he worries me now. I've planned too carefully to want a stumbling block."

"He's still only one man, Luke."

"One good man over there on the other side of the river could make a lot of difference. Cappy Lovett? He's a drunken, jug-sucking coward. Blount? A stupid fool who'll dig his own grave in the long run. Johnny? A crazy kid who'll get himself killed through his own craziness. But that stranger is of a different cut. I felt it last night. I felt it again tonight. And now he's riding for Diamond L."

Cultus gave him a careful look and said with the boldness of his years, "Luke, I think you're scared!"

"No," Ramage said. "Not scared. Just figuring to play it safe."

Cultus cocked his head again. "Sounds like Herb's coming back."

Again Ramage heard the clatter of hoofs in the yard, the hard strike of bootheels against the gallery flooring; and he moved his gun forward, thus showing Herb a greater respect than he had ever given the boy before. But it was a man who entered, a tall, angular, saturnine man who came into the room with the familiarity of one who belonged here. He stopped short to give his news.

"Hugh McCoy's dead," said Ringo.

"So?" Ramage said and showed neither sorrow nor elation. "Then Smeed called it right."

"Smeed went out to get his supper," Ringo said. "When he got back, he found McCoy gone."

"Then Hugh never came awake, even for a minute?"

"Not while Smeed was with him."

Cultus shook his head. "Hugh gone... It's hard to believe."

Ramage began pacing, moving to and fro across the room, his blocky face set, his thoughts far-reaching. At last he came to a stand. "Now Diamond L is outlaw," he said, his eyes showing his satisfaction. "Cultus, we'd best get out to the camp. I'm done with waiting. Ringo, I don't know whether to line you up openly with us or let you keep on playing a stray rider who hasn't signed up. What do you think?"

Ringo's fixed grin had been wiped away by that long hard ride from town, but it came back now. "I've got more news for you, Ramage. I'm not the only man from Pleasant Valley in the basin. I ran into another hand from Arizona tonight. One I saw you talking to just before you rode out."

Ramage's interest quickened. "You know him?'"

"Clint Tracy," Ringo said.

"Friend of yours?"

"I hate his guts!"

"Then," said Ramage, "your job is cut out for you. I want this Tracy dead."

"Dead?" Ringo repeated, and his grin broadened. "I haven't told you all of it. Sit down, Ramage. It looks like we've got some scheming to do."

7. The High Hills

THE TRAIL Beth Lovett and Clint Tracy took from Diamond L led due eastward over easy country, the two riding stirrup to stirrup across a land that glimmered faintly in the starshine. Not many minutes out of the ranch-yard, Beth turned north. Tracy voiced surprise, but Beth said, "There's a ford across the Thief up here."

Tracy came along silently then, glad to lean upon her knowledge of the country. He had braved the river last night, having little choice, and he was glad to hear of the ford. The memory was still strong in him of the swift pull of the Thief's current, the strangling moment when he had gone to the bottom. The river was an enemy with sinister ways, an alien thing to a man schooled to the land. He was afraid of the river and unashamed of his fear. They rode along with the willows at their right hand and were sometimes lost in the shadows of the willows. The river's turbulent song was in Tracy's ears constantly.

At the ford the river was a sheet of dull silver with the stars showing upon a placid surface. The river's song was muted to mere murmur, and peace lay all around. Here a sylvan hush made the night friendly, blunting wariness. But as they neared an open place in the willows, Tracy suddenly reached and jerked at the bridle of Beth's horse, quickly moving both horses into the deeper shadows.

Beth asked softly, "What is it?"

"Quiet!" he said.

His fingers closed on her arm, further cautioning her to silence. He rose in his stirrups and leaned forward intently, listening for whatever sound had brought a warning to him. Then the sound became big in the night, the beat of hoofs coming out of the north, from the direction of Spurlock. Tracy came down from the saddle, clamping his free hand over his horse's nostrils. He saw Beth alight, too, and they stood thus, silent and ready.

After that, Tracy saw movement. A small knot of riders angled abruptly toward the ford but reined up and made a dark, huddled mass. Tracy dropped the reins and got his gun into his hand, certain that he and Beth had been sighted.

From the group came a cautious, "Hallo—?"

Still the two held silent, and someone called then, "Broken Box—?" the voice blurred by whiskey.

"Easy!" Tracy whispered to Beth.

A shadow detached itself from the group and moved forward, covering half the distance between the others and the place where Tracy and Beth stood. This rider asked, "Who's there?" His voice held the self-consciousness of one who speaks with no sure knowledge that anyone listens. He hesitated a moment and seemed to be peering hard, then wheeled his mount about and rejoined the group. There was low muttered talk; and then the horses moved to a walk, splashed into the river, and began their crossing.

Beth whispered, "Can you make them out?"

The willows formed a screen through which the river showed dimly. Tracy strained his eyes. "Three—four of them," he judged. "Maybe five."

Beth expelled her breath. "That was a mighty tight thing while it lasted."

Tracy nodded. "They weren't very sure they saw anybody or they'd have taken a closer look. I'd guess they'd been having a high time in town. Whiskey blunted their edge."

Beth said, "You mentioned talking to Luke Ramage. Was Broken Box in Spurlock?"

"I saw Ramage and that kid, Herb. There may have been more. A heap of horses were at the hitchrails. I couldn't check all the brands." He lifted himself to the saddle. "We'll give them a couple more minutes head start, then cross over."

Beth mounted, too. She held silent a moment, then said, "There's something you should know." She told him of her earlier crossing of the ford and her rendezvous with Johnny and the clash they'd had with the two riders who'd found them on Broken Box land.

Tracy listened attentively, remembering how in Diamond L's parlor he had been struck with the certainty that something had happened to her in the early evening, something that had made her receptive to his proposal that they get Johnny to surrender himself. Now he said, "You're thinking that yonder bunch may be on the prowl for Johnny. Is that what's worrying you?"

"I just don't know." Her voice shook. "I've had all this time to wonder whether Johnny is lying dead over there somewhere."

Tracy said soothingly, "This bunch just came from town. All the sign says so. But just to play safe, we'll give them a good long start."

A full fifteen minutes they loitered; and when he signaled the start by jogging his horse, he came into the river with the feeling that he and Beth were now naked to any guns that might be waiting in the willows on the far bank. But they crossed without incident. The water reached no higher than their stirrups; the night's peace stayed unbroken. When they'd got through the willows and were riding upon Broken Box land, Tracy pulled up again and sat listening. Far out and away was the dwindling echo of moving horses, the vague rumor of men traveling.

Beth said, "You guessed there might be five. I'd say there were only two riding now."

He considerd this; it was very important. He strained his ears harder, his head sharply canted; he pitted himself against distance, trying to wring from the illusive murmurs of sound a true story. But the beating rhythm, growing more remote, became lost.

"Maybe they split," he said. "Or maybe they weren't all Broken Box and some of them headed north again, once they were across the river."

Beth noded. She was somber faced in the starlight. "There are other ranches over here."

Tracy smiled. "We'd better hurry along. We don't want daylight to find us on Broken Box."

"No," Beth said, and moved half-a-horse ahead, leading the way.

He was content to trust her judgment and follow. He had found her capable at all things to which she turned her hand and her mind. Off yonder somewhere in this immensity of night and sky and hill-hemmed land lay Broken Box's headquarters and Broken Box's roundup camp, and he had no wish to blunder into either. But if he saw them on that ride, it was only as lights in the distance, and even then he couldn't be sure. He had been too harried last night to get an accurate idea of this side of the Thief.

Presently they came upon the huge pile of rocks where Beth had had her misadventure of a few hours earlier. She said, "This is it," and slowed her horse to a walk, Tracy following suit. They skirted the place warily, and once beyond it, lifted their mounts to a gallop.

The basin's eastern walls bulked ahead of them, rearing larger as the two thundered away the miles. The far cry of coyotes came out of the night, growing sharper as they neared the hills. Riding like this, Tracy sensed always the closeness of Beth. She was a silent spirit with whom his destiny was now entwined; yet he was alone, too, as alone as he'd been on the long trail up out of Arizona and over all that long trail that had been his life. In such moments his thoughts soared free, and the bigness of the prairies and the mountains and the wide sky was a mystery almost solved. The thing to which he had committed himself now made sense, and he was glad for tonight's riding.

The country was growing steadily rougher, the slopes having a steeper pitch; and half of what had been left of the night was gone when they got into the hills. Now the terrain was as it had been at the Notch, to the south, the trail spongy with needle fall and the hills making their own kind of prison, with only the sky open above. And sometimes the sky was nearly shut off by overlocking branches, and they rode through layering darkness.

Up here there were game trails and cattle trails and the crumbling ruts of roads long unused, a senseless crisscrossing maze. Tracy would soon have been lost but for Beth. They rode single-file, the girl's voice drifting back to warn him of low-hanging branches or abrupt turns. They climbed steadily, the horses laboring.

Sometimes the hill broke into grassy benches, this openness making the return to timbered trails the more oppressive. Gulches gouged the hill's side, and the wind that flowed down from the summit had the breath of winter in it, so that Tracy wished he wore heavier clothes.

He was growing weary of the riding and the climbing when Beth led the way into the maw of a gulch. At first they moved in utter darkness in which he was strongly conscious that a creek flowed somewhere near at hand. He had to call out softly to Beth to be sure of her whereabouts. Her voice drifted back to him, soft and reassuring. The the gulch broadened, and the creek he'd heard caught the starshine. Tracy faintly discerned a huddle of ancient shacks and cabins strewed along either slope of the gulch, with the creek running between, brawling over rocks and finding its sinuous way downhill. Farther up, above the buildings, the dark of timber showed.

"This is Orlando," Beth said.

This was not the first ghost-town he had seen in these Montana hills. They were all alike, crumbling coffins for hopes long dead, towns that had boomed briefly until the will-o'-the-wisp of a greater strike had drawn their populations elsewhere overnight. Sometimes, he supposed, if the wind were right and a man's heart were tuned to it, you could hear the old laughter and the old frolicking, and perhaps the weeping, too, for some echo of these must have been left behind. But this town lay eerie and silent, no light showing, and its only life the small, unseen life that rattled its claws upon the rocks, its only voice the creek's turbulent one. In the hush, Beth's voice became a startling thing as she cupped her hands to her mouth and cried, "Johnny? Where are you, Johnny?"

The gulch's sides caught her voice and fashioned it into echoes, flinging these into abandoned corners until far ghosts were calling, "Johnny? Where are you, Johnny?" in dwindling, dying voices. Beth waited, tense in her saddle; and Tracy knew the run of her thoughts. Had Johnny managed to return to this hill hideout? Or had Broken Box trapped him on the basin's floor tonight?

Now Tracy could distinguish one building from another in the haphazard, straggly street; and he saw a tottering structure of log and frame that had once been a saloon, the only two-storied building in Orlando. Its windows were dead, empty eyes. From one of these, above the rotting wooden overhang of the porch, a voice said cautiously, "Beth! Come up here and put your horse out of sight around back. Say, who's that with you?"

"A friend," Beth said.

"I can't seem to make him out. You sure he's all right?"

"I'm sure, Johnny."

She and Tracy dismounted and led their horses up the gulch slope, making a tortuous ascent; for rotting sluice boxes littered the ground, and they had to pick their way around a flume which had once spanned the gulch but had fallen from its support to lie broken. After a stiff climb, they groped behind the saloon and found a horse tethered.

A door creaked in the banked shadows. Johnny Lovett said, "In here." He was no more than a voice to Tracy; then a light blossomed as Johnny ran his thumb along a match head. "Stairs to your right," Johnny said. "It's creaky, but it will hold you."

He held the match high, and Tracy saw that Johnny had his sister's yellow hair and fineness of features, but Tracy sensed him to be higher strung, lacking her cool practicality and her steadfastness.

Johnny held the match a second longer than was necessary, having a look at Tracy; and Beth said, "This is Clint Tracy, a new hand."

"The drifter you mentioned?"

"Yes," Beth said.

"Couldn't you have come with Corb or one of the regular hands?"

"I had my reasons," Beth said.

Johnny grunted. They groped their way up the stairs and along a dark tunnel of a hall to a room at the front of this second story. Here, with a little starlight showing through the window overlooking the gulch, Tracy dimly made out spread blankets. Ancient dust lay everywhere, rising chokingly where it had been disturbed by their passage. All the odors of abandonment mingled in a single smell, pervasive and stifling. The window had long since lost its oiled deerskin pane, and Tracy relished the night air.

Johnny spoke to his sister. "You got home okay?"

"Broken Box chased you instead of me."

Johnny laughed. "They couldn't have caught a spavined cow, those rannyhans, and they didn't have a plugged peso's worth of fight in 'em. All they wanted to do was make a big racket and a show of stirring the dust. You savvy? Their game was to chase me without getting too close. When I got tired of that kind of frolicking, I left them running in circles and cut for the hills."

Beth said testily, "I didn't find it such a lark, Johnny."

Johnny's voice sobered. "I reckon not. I was working at drawing 'em away from you. Don't think I haven't been worried since. I even thought of heading for the ranch to make sure about you." He hunkered down. "What fetched you again, Beth?"

Clint Tracy had listened silently, trying to measure Johnny Lovett; and it was his judgment that Johnny's bravado was mostly show, an effort to hide a genuine concern that had shadowed him ever since he'd parted from his sister at the rock pile. Yet it was also his feeling that Johnny needed a stiff shock; so Tracy answered for Beth, saying, "Hugh McCoy died tonight, Johnny."

Johnny sucked in his breath, hard hit by this. His voice came cold and distant. "Did that have to bring you here in the middle of the night? Couldn't the news have kept till daylight?"

"We want you to surrender to Harriman," Beth said. "The sooner the better."

Johnny gave this short consideration. "I won't do it!"

"Look," Tracy asked, "what have they got against you that could move a jury?"

Johnny said, "It's no secret that I said plenty about McCoy. Then he got shot from cover. The day that happened I was riding the range maybe ten, twenty miles away. A little job of fixing fence. But only my horse could testify to that. He doesn't talk."

Tracy said, "If you can't prove you weren't around Broken Box, at least nobody can prove you were."

"Mister," Johnny said, "you're a damn' fool!"

Temper stirred in Tracy; but he said evenly, "Sure, I know it isn't as simple as that. You're thinking that you could be framed. Broken Box could swear in witnesses who'd claim they saw you pull the trigger. But that isn't the way Broken Box wants it played. They'd rather you kept on hiding, Johnny. For that's all they need in the way of excuse to bring their war right into Diamond L's yard. And you didn't help any tonight when you started slamming bullets at those Broken Box boys!"

Johnny said, "You're a new face around this range. You must have figured things out quick."

Here was Corb Blount's own suspicion, voiced by another man; and Tracy had nothing with which to allay it. So he only said, "It's the facts that count, kid, not the man who speaks them."

Johnny said, "I'm staying in the hills till Tripp comes home."

Beth cried out, "Can't either you or Dad think of anybody but Tripp?"

Johnny stood up and took a quick turn acoss the room and back, a cat's restlessness in him, the old floor squealing to his boots. "Never you mind, Beth. Tripp and me will make a pair of aces back to back. Watch Ramage curl when he bucks that combination."

Beth said to Tracy in a weary voice, "Tripp's our older brother. He couldn't pass a card game or a bar or a pretty face. Everything he did had flash to it. He started his show first thing in the morning, when he took the kinks out of his horse. He was still at it when he hauled off his boots at night. The whole basin just didn't make enough elbow room for Tripp. He pulled out for Texas about two years ago. Dad sent him a letter since then. I guess you've seen that Dad is living for Tripp's return. And so is Johnny."

Tracy said, "Suppose that letter is lying unclaimed in some Texas post office? Suppose Tripp rode a thousand miles farther?"

"Hell," Johnny said, "you don't know Tripp. He'll show home sooner or later."

Tracy's mind went back to the restaurant in Spurlock and Tripp's name penciled on the wall, and his thought there that Tripp Lovett was everywhere in this basin. The man's shadow was indeed a long one, stretching from Diamond L's gallery, where Cappy Lovett sat with his telescope and his jug, to these high hills where another Lovett also waited. He sensed that logic would no more touch Johnny than it had his father, not where Tripp Lovett was involved. He said, "You just can't count on Tripp. Here's the real choice: you can stay here, and that makes Diamond

L an outlaw outfit; or you can ride back with us. Now which is it going to be?"

Johnny moved to the window and put his shoulder against its rotted frame. He said in a tight, belligerent voice, "If I ride out of here, it will be to Broken Box's door to call Ramage into the yard. If McCoy's dead, then Ramage is Broken Box. So that's the way to settle it—a Broken Box man and a Diamond L man looking at each other through gunsmoke. That's how Tripp would do it."

Beth said, "That's all he's got in his head! Gunplay! I'm beginning to hate the name of Tripp Lovett!"

She was a small, indistinct shape; yet suddenly she was clearer in Tracy's eyes than she had been before. Now he understood her aloofness which had closed him out at their first meeting, and he also knew what had forced her decision to fetch him here to Orlando tonight. It was painfully clear. Earlier she had asked him to ride off Diamond L forever, and that had been because of his feverish talk of Pleasant Valley. She had wanted no gunman around for Johnny Lovett to ape. She had had one wildling brother and watched him ride away; and now that Johnny was another Tripp Lovett in the making, she was trying to hold him from the violent trails.

A Cappy Lovett could dream of a Tripp Lovett shaped to his own idealistic fancy; a Corb Blount could think only of cattle and a man's right to defend his own brand. Beth had been the one fighting the real fight.

Knowing this, Tracy was suddenly done with reasonableness, for there was only one kind of persuasion for Johnny. He said, "Look at me, kid!"

But Johnny didn't turn his head. He was staring through the window, and he kept his gaze bent that way.

"I've got my gun out and lined on you, Johnny," Tracy said. "No, don't reach. You're against the light; I'm in shadow. You're going with us—you're going all the way to Harriman's jail with a gun at your back, if need be. But it will be a Diamond L gun. I think the rest of the basin will remember that and count the difference for what it's worth."

A cry rose in Beth's throat; but Tracy said gently, "Can't you see there is no other way?"

"Yes," she said. "I guess so."

Johnny laughed in a low voice. "This is really funny!"

"No," Tracy said, "you're wrong about that, Johnny."

"You don't savvy," Johnny said. "Somebody moved out there, across the gulch. I've been watching him these last few minutes, making sure. Now I've spotted two of them. You were careless, friend. Broken Box followed you here."

Tracy moved quickly toward the window, the certainty leaping in him that this could be no ruse of Johnny's. He, Tracy, had been right at the Thief's ford when he'd judged that four or five men had crossed. But Beth had been right, too, when she'd thought that only two men had ridden on toward Broken Box. Now Tray understood. At least two of those riders had waited on the far bank, not to ambush him and Beth from the willows as they might have done but to follow them afterwards. And so they had been trailed to this, their destination.

8. Hemmed In

IN THE darkness Beth moved softly, then brushed close to Tracy beside the window. He felt the rigidity of her body; and her voice was strained and desperate, edged with fatigue and fear. She said, "Having Broken Box take him to Harriman wouldn't be the same thing."

Knowing she would want the truth, Tracy said, "Likely Broken Box wouldn't bother. That brand of theirs is shaped like a gallows. My guess is that they'd use a rope and the handiest tree."

She sucked in her breath sharply. "You're probably right."

"No pie till they catch their rabbit," Johnny observed; but his bravado fell short of full conviction.

Tracy peered down the gulch, being careful not to expose himself. He saw only banked shadows and the faint reflection of starshine on the mountain creek. Across the way, the buildings were a dark huddle, formless and silent. All things were deceptive in the meager light. His eyes ached with staring. He began to fancy movement everywhere and shook his head to rid himself of the illusion.

"We can fight or run," he said.

"We fight!" Johnny decided.

Tracy thought a moment. "No," he said, "we run. I blundered once tonight when I let them cut sign on us. We'll not play into their hands again. It must be that they didn't open up on us from the willows because you were along, Beth. Or maybe, once they recognized us as Diamond L, they figured it smarter to trail us. When we headed into the hills, they guessed Johnny was up here. What else would have been taking us on such a trail? I'll bet that one of them is riding back to Broken Box right now. That means we'll have the whole crew hitting the saddle."

"They won't make it here till mid-morning," Johnny observed. "It's still a couple of hours till sunup."

"Then let's not waste those hours cruising around down there in the gulch shooting at shadows," Tracy insisted. "Man, don't you see that Hugh McCoy's dying makes the difference? Broken Box has likely got that news by now. Ramage can hunt you to the ends of the earth!"

"And he'll do it," Beth said firmly.

"Then if I've got to make a stand against him," Johnny said, "it might as well be right here."

Tracy's temper overpowered him. "You damn' fool, your sister's here! Are you always going to be picking fights and leaving her to face the bullets?"

This reached through to Johnny. He held silent for a moment, then said soberly, "I didn't think."

Tracy turned to Beth. "Is there a back trail out of here?"

Her face was a smudge in the darkness. "If you want to call it that," she said.

Johnny knelt and began rolling up his blankets; but Tracy said impatiently, "Never mind those! We'll want to travel light and fast."

Beth said, "We'll take the grub." She began groping in the corners until she lifted a muslin sack bulging with canned goods.

This was the one she'd fetched from Diamond L earlier tonight, Tracy judged. He took it from her hands and passed it to Johnny. "Here, pack this," he said. He'd noticed that Beth's hands trembled. It had been a mighty hard night for her.

Then Tracy stepped toward the door, saying, "Easy now."

They got into that tunnel of a hall and groped along it to the creaky stairs and began the descent. The smell of dust grew strong, and it seemed to Tracy that their passage must be sending its own warning to all the corners of Orlando, for the stairs squealed with their combined weight. Something scurried in the lower darkness, and again he heard Beth suck in her breath sharply. "A rat," Tracy whispered.

He was in the lead. Suddenly he thrust out both arms, barring the other two. He had reached the bottom of the stairs, and the three stood rigid while Tracy keened the darkness for whatever intangible had first disturbed him. He had learned to heed small warnings and to place his trust in instinct; this was the training of Pleasant Valley, and it had become ingrained. He waited out an endless moment, the feeling strong in him that someone else was not in this building. Then a bootsole scraped in the vastness of the barroom; and a gun blossomed in the darkness, the thunder of it multiplied by the confining walls.

Crouching low and throwing a shot in the direction of the gunflame, Tracy shouted, "Outside! Quick! Johnny, take care of her!"

Boots pounded in the blind depths of the room. Johnny moved past Tracy and got the back door open and was murkily silhouetted for a second. Tracy fired again, once, twice, a third time, blending the shots in a single roll of sound and sweeping his gun-barrel in a wide arc. He was seeking no target; he wanted only to throw panic into that hidden gunman before the fellow could line his sights on the rear doorway.

Beth got through, but still Tracy lingered. He hunkered down, quiet and attentive. The smell of powdersmoke was heavy in the air; the hidden foe was as quiet as Tracy, waiting in darkness, waiting his chance. Tracy risked reloading his gun, hurrying the job. Then he stood up and darted through the doorway. His movement brought the hidden gun to life. A bullet drove a splinter from the door frame, but Tracy had got outside.

He swung around, his gun ready if the Broken Box man were so foolish as to follow him. Johnny had kept his horse saddled and had only to tighten the cinch, so he was mounted and struggling to tie the grub sack to his saddle horn. Beth, too, was mounted. Tracy was the last into leather.

All the night's silence lay shattered. Boots pounded across ancient planking, and a voice called, "Snap! Speak up! Where the hell are you?"

Tracy got his horse wheeled about and let Beth take the lead. He motioned for Johnny to follow her. Tracy brought up the rear, his body half-turned in the saddle, his gun held ready, and every sense alert to danger.

That lost voice called again, "Snap! Where are you, man?" A gun opened up somewhere in the shadows, and that was Snap's way of speaking.

Tracy remembered Snap. He'd been the one with an oldster's weary voice who'd lain hidden across the trail when Herb had trapped Tracy at the Notch. It crossed Tracy's mind that this was the second time he'd met up with Snap, yet he'd never seen the man's face.

Then his horse was laboring along a steep, black trail, climbing. Tracy had a last glimpse of the rooftops of Orlando, touched with silver by starshine, before timber closed around the trail, a thick stand of lodgepole. He had to trust to his horse and run in smothering darkness, following Johnny and Beth. Someone below was still throwing shots; they were wild shots, made of frustration and anger. Soon even the sound of them was lost; and Tracy could hear the wind that threaded through the treetops, that and the creak of saddle leather and the jingle of bit chains. Presently the trail leveled off and became a black shelf on the slope.

Beth called back, "Slow to a walk."

Tracy was glad of this, not liking blind riding along an unknown trail on a horse he wasn't used to. They moved slowly, still strung out but no longer climbing. They rode like this for a half hour, and then Beth called, "Pull up."

From the feel of wind moving across openness, Tracy sensed they had come into some kind of mountain meadow. The wind had a promise of winter in it, and again Tracy wished for heavier clothes. With most of the stars gone and the dawn not yet showing, the darkness had grown impenetrable. The three huddled together here, and Beth said, "No pursuit, it seems. We might as well wait for morning."

Tracy tried hard to pierce the darkness. "Where does this trail lead?"

"Northward along the shoulder of the hills. After a while it crosses the railroad tracks. Spurlock is due west from there."

Johnny said, "I've hunted up here. Tripp used to take me with him when I was stirrup high."

"Broken Box know this country?"

"They must," Beth said. "They summer graze in these hills, though not this high up."

Tracy was busy at drawing a mental map; the picture it brought made him frown. "One of them—Snap, or the other fellow—could stay at Orlando, cutting us off from behind. The other could head back and meet Broken Box and give them the word. Assuming that the outfit is already on the way, what's to keep Ramage from cutting north along the base of the hills? He could be ready and laying for us at the end of this trail."

"That's true," Beth said. "But it had to be this—or stay in Orlando. We can't cut directly down the slope, not with horses. The timber's too thick, and there are drop-offs. And we can't make time in this darkness and hope to outflank Ramage, if your guess is right. It was the choice of the frying pan or the fire."

She'd been thinking of Johnny again, Tracy knew, and had backed his own choice to run instead of fight only because it delayed the inevitable. Give Johnny too much taste for gunsmoke and you had another Tripp Lovett in the family. But there was more than that to it. Again Tracy thought of Cappy Lovett, with his telescope and his forlorn hope, and of Corb Blount, whose stubborn loyalty could hold the seeds of disaster for Diamond L. He thought of Johnny Lovett, a straw in a troublesome wind; and an earlier conviction strengthened in him. The fight that Beth was making was the important one—she fought for the future of all of them.

He said gently, "We might as well light down and rest." Dismounting, he began tugging off saddle and blanket. "Johnny, we'll take turns guarding the backtrail."

"Sure," Johnny said.

At Orlando Tracy had pitted himself against Johnny, drawing a gun in desperation; but now they were allied in a common cause. This gave Tracy no choice but to trust the boy. He let Johnny take the first watch; Johnny drifted off into the darkness and was soon lost to sight. Tracy spread the blankets and said, "Beth, here's your bed." He stretched himself nearby, his mind fuzzy and his body tired.

He felt hands at his shoulder; and Beth said, "Here, put one of these blankets under that wound. I shan't need both of them."

He said, "Thank you," too drowsy to protest.

She moved back to her improvised bed and her voice drifted to him. "Thank you, too, Clint," she said. "Thank you a lot." He wondered exactly what she was thanking him for, and wondering, he fell asleep...

The pressure of Johnny's hand on his good shoulder awoke him, and he sat up. Brittle morning light made him blink. He saw the grassy expanse of the mountain meadow, and the timber walling it; to the north the crest of a higher hill showed, brown and bare. He heard the faraway music of that same creek that brawled through Orlando in its downward drop to join the Thief. He built a cigarette, and it was the first one that had tasted good to him lately. He noticed that Beth was up and about. His shoulder was stiff. This worried him; and he moved his arm like the piston of a locomotive, loosening up his muscles.

He looked up at Johnny. "That was one damn' short watch I had last night, kid."

Johnny said, "I let you sleep. About all I've done lately is sleep."

Tracy nodded. He had his first real look at Johnny now, seeing the golden stubble on Johnny's cheeks and jaw and upper lip. There was a cat-nervousness about Johnny always; he was a boy filled with vast energies and no sure knowledge of how to use them. His temper, Tracy now knew, lay close to the surface and was as quick as his smile. Looking at him, Tracy remembered Broken Box's Herb standing on the porch of the Argonaut, having in him the markings for a good life or a wild one. Johnny, too, was poised like that at a crossroads; and Johnny was Tripp Lovett's brother.

Beth broke Tracy's train of thought. "It had best be a cold breakfast," she said. "If anyone followed from Orlando, we don't want smoke to point the way."

"Breakfast..." Tracy said. "Now there's a good word."

Beth busied herself with canned goods from the grub sack, borrowing a knife from Johnny. After they'd eaten, she said, "I've been thinking. If we're hemmed in, with the trail cut off at both ends, perhaps we might best stay here till twilight. Maybe by then they'll have tired of waiting for us. After all, they've got a roundup to think about. We can start riding before it gets too late and have darkness to protect us if we have to run a gantlet."

Johnny at once showed petulance. "Unless they come closing in on us meanwhile."

"Then why wear out our horses riding to meet them?"

"She's right," Tracy said. "Besides, if we don't show up, they may figure that we've risked cutting down the slope."

Thus it was decided, though anything that meant inactivity was wearing upon Johnny; and he showed a hard frown at the prospect. The sun climbed high enough to reach down through the treetops, dispelling the last fog wisps clinging about the summits. They moved the horses into the timber but didn't saddle them. The day wore on; they ate again, but sparingly, not knowing how long the food might have to last. They wandered about, keeping always alert for whatever might show on the trail. It would have been an idyllic day except for their tension.

In mid-afternoon, Tracy, lazing upon one of the blankets, said to Beth, "What about Corb Blount? Will he fetch the crew out, since we haven't showed back?"

She took a moment before answering, and he got the impression that she carefully weighed the matter first. "Corb has been with Diamond L since before I was born," she said. "I have never known him to tell a lie or use an oath or change his mind once it was set. He thought I was a fool to trust you, but I stuck by my choice. I forfeited his help when I went against his judgment. No, he'll not be fetching the crew. Unless Dad should give him a direct order to come looking."

Tracy said, "Blount's a strange man."

"Maybe you don't understand," she said. "If harm should come to me or Johnny because of you, Corb would follow you all the way back to Arizona for an accounting. When he warned you about that, he meant it."

Tracy said again, "A strange man..."

He lay back upon the blanket; from the corner of an eye he watched the horses crop grass. He heard Beth move off and begin talking to Johnny. Their voices became a blur, an endlessness of sound without meaning; and soon he slept again...

Thus the long day spun itself out, and in the last of its light they saddled and continued northward.

Nearly always, once the meadow was behind them, the trail was a pine-shrouded tunnel, narrow and sinuous. Sometimes they came upon other meadows; and at places the timber thinned, and they looked down upon the basin floor spread golden with sunset, a distant panorama soft-hued in the afterglow. When the darkness came, pinpoints of light sprang up on the velvet spaces, and Spurlock was nearer with each showing. A taut wariness began to grip Tracy. The long day had worn at his nerves; and he was edgy with the thought that since Broken Box hadn't showed, Broken Box would likely be waiting.

In the early evening they reached the railroad tracks and turned, single-filing westward and downward as they paralleled the embankment wherever the terrain permitted. Tracy was struck by an idea then. "Tell me, is there a train due along here?" he asked.

Startled, Beth said, "Why, yes. I think so. It's Wednesday, isn't it? The freight should come through about ten." She glanced at Johnny for confirmation.

Tracy said, "That will do it. We'll leave the horses. They'll find their way back to Diamond L. All we've got to do is grab that freight and ride it into Spurlock. Right past anybody who's waiting below."

Johnny shouted his enthusiasm. "All day we've waited to ride to these tracks, but nobody thought of catching a train! Ain't that something!"

Tracy looked hard at him, knowing that now the test must come and still not being sure about Johnny. "Harriman should be in Spurlock, boy."

A great good humor filled Johnny, and he gave Tracy a lopsided grin. "So he should. Badge and all. You figgering to pull that gun again, mister?"

"If I have to," Tracy said, not smiling.

Johnny's grin grew wider. "Hell, I thought it all over while I was doing the guarding early this morning. Then Beth and I talked about it while you were snoozing this afternoon. I'm not solid tallow between the ears. She showed me the light. You were right. I'm only giving Broken Box the edge if I stay hiding. So let's go call on Harriman."

"That's fine," Tracy said.

Beth said, "You'll be sorry, Johnny."

Tracy glanced at her and saw a great calmness upon her.

Johnny had wisdom in him after all, given the time for the wisdom to come out, Tracy reflected. He remembered those two portraits in the Diamond L parlor; he remembered the firmness of the woman's chin. That, too, was Johnny's heritage. Tracy had a feeling of achievement different from anything he'd ever known, and a gladness beyond explaining. To cover this, he said gruffly, "Now we've got to wait out that freight."

They chose a point farther down, where the railroad swung around a sharp curve; for here any train would have to slacken speed. They waited while the night grew to fullness and the first stars appeared, the treetops standing ragged against them. Time dragged endlessly; and then a locomotive mourned in the hills, its lonesome whistle drifting down.

"Here she comes," Johnny cried.

When they heard the first faint throbbing of the rails, they dismounted, hung bridles upon the saddle horns, and slapped the mounts in the direction of home, watching until the timber claimed the horses.

Tracy glanced at Beth. "You ready?"

The beam of a locomotive swept around the curve, bathing them briefly in its light. The locomotive thundered by, and the long string of freight cars began rolling past. "Now!" Tracy shouted. They ran for it, snatching at the iron ladders and clambering upward. Tracy gave Beth a hand and saw her laughing with the adventure of this.

The three met atop the cars, and Johnny eased to the edge of one and sat down and joyously swung his feet. He was all boy in this free moment, but Tracy came over and pulled at his arm. "Flatten out," Tracy said. "We may have friends waiting below."

They lay prone; Tracy tugged hard at his hat, jamming it tight. The train swung down the hillside; timber and bushes beyond the embankment became a blur. Cinders strung them, and the wind pulled at the three, and they had to raise their voices above it when they spoke. They rolled on for a mile and another. The train had almost reached the floor of the basin when Beth cried, "There they are!"

Tracy saw them, a huddle of cowboys, nearly a dozen, standing ready beside their horses in a grove of trees, the bigness of Luke Ramage bulking among them. At the same moment someone spied the three atop the car. The fellow pointed and shouted, a cry going up from Broken Box that was not quite lost in the clacking of the wheels, the groaning of the cars. One lifted a gun and fired; the flame smeared redness across the night. Someone brandished a fist; a second gun spoke.

Johnny was jerking at his own weapon, his face angry. He leveled his gun, then tilted it downward; but Tracy instantly clamped hard fingers on Johnny's wrist. He wrenched Johnny's hand aside. Johnny cursed him and struggled to free himself, but by then Broken Box was lost from their sight.

Johnny said, "Just one shot! All I wanted was one shot!"

Tracy said, "Didn't you see? Hap Harriman was with them! If you'd shot, you'd have been shooting at him, too. He's with them, I tell you! Now why is that?"

9. Hit the Saddle!

OF THE many cruising shadows that were Broken Box men riding through the night which had brought Beth Lovett and Clint Tracy to Orlando, one rode with his pride galled and his anger great. And that one was Herb.

Heading south from Broken Box's headquarters after his set-to with Luke Ramage, he had galloped hard, the echo of Ramage's voice in his ears, the feel of Ramage's fingers still stinging his cheek. He had known no depth of spirit lower than this. He wept, his mind turning to murder; but there was no death for Ramage that would have satisfied Herb, not even the kind the Indians dealt out. Death was to easy. Damned if it wasn't!

He cursed Ramage in a high, shrill voice that he hurled against the empty night, venting his anger with spur and quirt upon the horse. Finally his breath was spent, and a measure of sanity came back to him, and he slowed his mount to a walk. Now that he stopped to think about it, he didn't want to get to the roundup camp too soon. Not while the crew was still up and about.

All day long Herb had fancied himself in a role to his liking; he had been a fighter among fighters, one who'd notched his gun and could therefore throw a wide shadow. He had liked this role, wringing from it a full measure of glory. By many means he'd brought the small talk of the crew around to the night before and so again given his account of the moment when he'd knocked the drifter from his horse into the raging Thief. The tale had grown with each telling, making Herb a braver man and a more resourceful one. He had drunk a heady draught, liking the taste of it. But he had bitterness in his mouth now.

True, only Cultus had witnessed what had happened at the ranch-house, and Cultus was not the talking kind. The crew might never know what Luke Ramage had done, but sooner or later word would reach camp that the drifter was still alive. Now that Herb turned the matter over in his mind, it struck him that some of the hands had been too eager to hear him out today, prompting him and asking pointed questions. Damn them, they hadn't believed him really! They'd been egging him on and laughing behind their whiskers all the while. He knew what kind of hoorawing he'd get when the myth exploded. And so his soul cringed with the prospect of facing them tonight.

All his life he'd wanted to ride stirrup to stirrup with the hard ones, standing equal in their eyes, being of their salty breed and having the respect one fighting man gives another. In his few years of drifting, he had never attained such stature, save for today; and his pride had grown starved and his spirit vicious. He'd had his brief taste of dream-come-true, and now the dream had been snatched from him. Tonight he'd touched the bottom of humiliation. And so the thought grew that he could just ride on, heading down through the Notch and out of the basin. That's what he could do.

But he didn't have the courage for that. He had known the lean belly and the roofless bed in his day. Fall roundups would be finished on most of the ranges, and ranch owners would be cutting down their crews. Remembering, he knew what it would be like. Too many cattlemen had looked at that pasty face and shaken their heads in other days; too many had given him a month's tryout and let him go. Only at Broken Box had he lasted.

Thus he now gravitated to Broken Box's camp as a horse gravitates to its corral, knowing numbly that here alone was security of a sort. Riding in, he put his mount in the remuda and approached the fire. Any hope he'd held that the crew would be rolled into tarps and asleep was blasted, for several sat about the blaze.

One of these was George, who'd fetched the chuck-wagon back. Two others were Sherm and Fletch, who'd been in Spurlock earlier in the evening and left town long before Herb. These two were re-telling the tale of an encounter at the rock pile with Johnny Lovett; but Herb lingered back in the shadows, keeping out of the talk. Earlier he would have sneered, for Sherm and Fletch had brushed with the enemy and failed to tally. Now Herb squirmed with the fear that this new tale of guns in the night might bring the talk around to himself.

"Luke got back to the ranch," George said reflectively. "Reckon Cultus will have told him about Johnny Lovett's being on this side of the Thief. I hope we don't have to go looking for him tonight."

Sherm spied Herb. "Here's the kid. What's doing up at the ranch? The ramrod got something on his chest?"

"Ask him," Herb said and turned away.

Sherm said to the others, "Did you hear that? The kid's got so big across the britches all of a sudden that he can't even talk to us."

The cook, seated on the chuck-wagon's tongue, frowned at the cowboys. "If you rannyhans think you're gonna set around burnin' up my breakfast wood, you got another think comin'. Them that ain't nighthawkin' git to your blankets."

One by one they drifted to their tarps, and the fire burned low. Herb, bedded down, lay upon his back, gazing at the stars and hating the men around him. In the far hills, a coyote mourned; from the flats came the toneless singing of the nighthawks. This was the silent hour when a man found peace, but there was none for Herb.

He dreamed sleepless dreams; he pictured himself riding out of here and carving a hard name for himself on another range. He thought of how it would be when his reputation drifted back and reached the ears of those now sleeping about him. He'd admire to see their faces then! And the look they'd wear when he showed around again to let them see how he'd turned out... He had fashioned such dreams before, sometimes so vividly that he believed them; but tonight they brought him no balm. And so he nursed his hate and his frustration and fell asleep...

His awakening was violent, brought about by the earth's shuddering to hoofs; and his first thought was the awful one: *Stampede!* Fear was a coldness in his belly and a hot sweat on his face. The sky was a crowding blackness, the stars gone; and he knew that it was nearly dawn. He got himself on one elbow and saw the vague shapes of riders milling in the camp, but still he couldn't shake off that feeling of catastrophe.

Someone had dismounted and was stirring the fire to life, recklessly heaping the cook's hoarded fuel upon it. The blaze sprang up, and in its spreading light Herb recognized all the horsemen. Four were Broken Box hands who'd still been in town when he'd left. Another was Cultus, and another was Ramage. But the surprising thing was that Sheriff Hap Harriman was with them, big and sloppy in his saddle.

"Roll out, all of you!" Ramage was roaring. "I want every man on his feet."

Suddenly the sweat was in Herb's eyes, blinding him. A great temptation tugged at him. He had his gun in his blankets; and there sat Ramage, a broad, fire-limned target. Herb's hate was such a brassy taste in his mouth as to leave him sick; his hate crowded all his consciousness. In his mind, he could hear himself saying, *"Ramage, there's a thing between us needs settling."* He had only to utter that challenge and let Ramage start drawing, and he could shoot Ramage now. In one brief play he could let all the world know that no man humiliated Herb and got away with it. He wanted nothing so much as he wanted Ramage dead.

Two things stayed his hand, and the moment was lost.

He remembered Ramage shooting the head off a rattlesnake with deadly accuracy not long ago. But the real hesitancy in Herb went deeper and was compounded of strange ingredients. He hated Ramage, yes. But Ramage was the toughest man he had ever known; and therefore he had tried patterning his ways after Ramage's, making himself a pale shadow of Ramage. For this man's approval he would have dared beyond daring. For this man's approval he had ridden recklessly ahead of the others last night and been the one to get close to that drifter. And now, hating Ramage, he still worshipped him; and thus to kill Ramage would be to kill part of himself.

He let his hand go from the gun under the blanket. He felt weak and used up, like someone who had walked near a brink in darkness, discovering his danger just in time.

All about him men were flinging their tarps aside, stomping into their boots, shouting sleepy questions. They came spilling into the firelight, Herb among them; they crowded around Ramage.

"I'll tell it quick," Ramage said. "I reckon you know that Sherm and Fletch found Johnny Lovett on this side of the river early tonight. Some of the boys came down from town later. At the ford, they thought somebody was hiding in the willows. They crossed over, but two of them stayed under cover while the rest rode on to give the idea that they'd all gone on. It was the Lovett girl and that drifter— his name's Clint Tracy—who came across the river. Yes, Tracy's still alive." His eyes sought out Herb, and he gave the boy his sour smile. "Herb just thought he got him. Ain't that so, Herb?"

Herb felt them all looking at him. Again words formed in his mind, but he said nothing.

"Snap and Pinto followed those two to Orlando," Ramage went on. "That's where Johnny Lovett's been holing up. Damned near under our noses!" His square face darkened with anger. "Snap's still there, but Pinto rode back with the word. He thinks those three from Diamond L cut back into the hills. We're going after them."

He looked around. "George, ride out and tell the nighthawks that they're to stay with the herd till we show back. It may be a day; it may be a week. Cook, you stay here, too. And you can get busy filling saddlebags with grub. The rest of you hit your saddles. We're going to head north and try to cut off Johnny Lovett."

Cultus had sat his saddle without speaking. A shadow crossed his face; and he said pointedly, "For God's sake, Luke, is that *all* the news you're going to tell 'em?"

"I see what you mean," Ramage said. "Boys, there's another thing. Hugh McCoy cashed in his chips early tonight. The sheriff here rode down to bring the news officially. He got a few hours' sleep in a Broken Box bunk, so he was around when Pinto rode in with the news about Johnny Lovett. Now Hap aims to ride along and see us catch a murderer."

Harriman said in an unsteady voice, "If you round up Johnny, he goes to jail."

He's scared! Herb thought, and he sneered, he who'd lived with fear all his days.

Ramage said, looking at Harriman and playing cat-and-mouse, "Maybe you'd better swear us all in as deputies, eh, Hap?"

Harriman said with a show of defiance, "There'll only be one badge needed after you've cornered him."

"Get gear onto the horses, boys!" Ramage shouted. "One of you head for the Notch and fetch back the guards. I want everybody riding."

Cultus said in his mild voice, "Don't you reckon somebody from this spread ought to go attend to Hugh?"

Ramage frowned. "Yeah, I suppose that's right." He looked over the men. "Herb, there's a job for you. Ride into Spurlock and get the funeral lined up. Tell Lundstrom that Broken Box wants the best coffin he's got in stock. Price don't mean a damn' thing. Tell him to hold up the planting till we show in town. You reckon you can do that chore without tangling your twine?"

Herb's slack mouth quivered. "Ah, hell, Luke—!"

"Get going!" Ramage snapped.

Herb moved slowly away, his face bleak. Some there were who would ride after Johnny Lovett and that drifter, Clint Tracy; and though the odds were all on Broken Box's side, there would be gunsmoke and a chance for a man to show his worth. Some would stay with the herd, but they would be the flimsy bulwark against the menace of Corb Blount's threatened Winchester cut; so these, too, might have their chance. Only one chore was the safe chore, and this was Herb's. And so he saddled up and rode out, his anger and humiliation greater than they had been before. He stood twice shamed and was sick with knowing how he must look to the others.

He had moved only a few yards from the roundup camp when Cultus drew up beside him. Herb gave him a hard stare. "What the hell do you want?" he demanded.

Cultus fished out the makings and spun himself a cigarette. "Smoke?"

"I've got my own."

"Look," Cultus said, jerking his head in the direction of the fire where Ramage still sat his saddle, "he had a bad time in town last night. He wasn't braced to find Clint Tracy walking around. That was your doin', kid."

Herb said doggedly, "Damn it, I saw him go into the river."

"Sure you did. But that ain't makin' Luke any less sore. He's a hard man, Herb; but he gives a fair shake when you've got one coming. You do something to shine in his eyes, and he'll notice it just as fast as he's noticed your mistakes. Meantime you've got to eat poor crow and like it. Thinkin' black thoughts won't help. Try showing Luke that you've got good stuff in you. That's the answer."

"Ah, hell!" Herb said and spat from the corner of his mouth.

"I was only aimin' to help get that burr out from under our saddle blanket," Cultus said mildly.

Herb made a sound in his throat and touched spurs to his horse.

He rode hard northward, again making his horse suffer, hating Cultus for his show of sympathy, hating being talked to as though he needed his nose wiped. At the ford he made a careful crossing, remembering that only Snap stood between the three from Diamond L and this means of returning to their home range. Anger gave him the same kind of courage whiskey did, and he hoped he'd be challenged. But the river lay peaceful in the spreading dawn, and no man disputed Herb's passage there or on the rest of the ride to Spurlock.

He reached town at an hour when the merchants were opening shutters and sweeping the boardwalks before their establishments, and pumps creaked as housewives began their day's doings. He put up his horse at the livery and had breakfast at Sally's and then he went to the furniture store to see Lundstrom about the coffin. Here some of yesterday's arrogance returned to him. Damned if he wasn't a man doing man's business, and he spoke for Broken Box as Luke Ramage would have spoken. After that there was a session with Smeed; and within the hour Hugh McCoy was lying in rude state in a back room of Lundstrom's establishment.

Herb stood looking down at the dead man, no real feeling in him. McCoy, alive, had been as remote as he was now, a distant spirit who abided Herb's presence only because Luke Ramage had insisted on hiring and keeping him. McCoy had been like those many others who had shaken their heads when Herb had ridden up asking for work. Herb had no tears for Hugh McCoy. The hell with him!

On the street again, Herb faced a long, empty day, for there was nothing to do but await the coming of Broken

Box from its mission in the hills. He gravitated to the Argonaut, finding the place deserted save for the swamper and the barkeep at this mid-morning hour. He got himself a deck of cards and took one of the tables and played endless solitaire, sometimes buying a drink. He had his noon meal at Sally's and returned to the cards again, but his hands grew less busy, and his mood turned sullen. He remembered himself and Tracy at the bank of the Thief. He remembered the wild uplift of spirit he had known when he'd seen the river claim Tracy. He cursed Tracy in his mind, seeing him now as the source of all his trouble.

Men drifted into the saloon during the afternoon, men of the other basin ranches, some giving him curt nods, some ignoring him. No one asked him to drink; and he wondered about that, his mood darkening. No one ever asked him to drink save those of his own crew.

Supper time came. When he'd finished eating, it was still early, but he had no more taste for the Argonaut and no more money to spend on drinks. He'd handed over his last fifty cent piece at the restaurant. He thought about bedding down. He'd had a broken night and felt sleepy, but he hadn't the price of a hotel room. Any other hand would have charged a room to Broken Box, but that might only give Ramage an excuse for anger. Herb headed for the livery. The hostler wasn't about, so he climbed to the loft and burrowed into the hay.

He lay sleepless for a long time, hearing the restless stomping of the horses below. Lamplight sprang into being, some of it seeping into the loft; and Herb discovered a large crack in the floor through which he could see the hostler moving about. He wanted no talk with the hostler or any man tonight, so he kept silent.

He had been pursuing a thought all day, following it down sluggish channels, a thought that had come of Cultus' talk. He'd seen the wisdom in Cultus' advice, but he'd been in no mood to be grateful. Yet the truth was there: he would be nothing in Luke Ramage's eyes until the chance came to balance an achievement against his failure.

If ever again he came up against Clint Tracy, he must be very sure that Tracy died.

Thinking this, Herb found it easy to transfer to Tracy the hate he'd felt for Ramage—that queer hate which was mixed with a blind worship for the only kind of strength Herb understood. He turned cold with the thought of Tracy, remembering their encounter at the Notch and afterwards; he turned hot with the terrible need to face Tracy again and kill him. He knew both fear and fury, wondering whether Broken Box had already overtaken Tracy and done for him, wondering if the chance could ever come his way again.

10. The One Who Waited

OUT OF the hills, the freight train that bore Clint Tracy and Johnny and Beth Lovett westward made good time across the flatlands, carrying them farther from the riders who'd waited at the foot of the hill trail. Tracy watched the night-softened landscape rush past and gauged the train's speed, matching it in his mind against running horses. Most likely Broken Box was long since into the saddle and hard after them. Or would Ramage attempt such an unequal race? Tracy frowned, glancing at the two seated beside him. Johnny showed a smoldering anger; Beth smiled tiredly.

"We'll soon be off this rattler," Tracy shouted.

Then Spurlock was ahead, a shapeless huddle upon the basin floor that grew in their vision and became a town. Tracy drew in a hard breath. The train rumbled over the railroad bridge spanning the Thief and slowed down near the loading chutes. Here, just outside Spurlock, the three alighted from the cars and stood stiffly, finding the solid ground uncertain to their feet. They came walking into town.

Tracy said, "We'll have to get hold of some horses;" but this was an absent statement, for his mind was busy with another thing. He was still wondering why Harriman had ridden with Broken Box tonight and what that portended. He said, flushing his real thinking to the surface, "Something's gone wrong," and shook his head. "Harriman..."

Beth touched his arm lightly. "It may not be what you suppose. Hap Harriman is not very brave or very wise, but I've always believed that he was just."

Johnny held his silence, trudging along with them, but his lips were still bleak and his eyes wary. Tracy guessed that Johnny was hard put to hold to his decision to surrender. Tracy had seen wild horses like that, laying back their ears and showing a lot of white in their eyes as the rope dragged them toward the corral.

Then they were into the main street and walking along it, and Spurlock seemed no different than it had the night before. Those whom they met upon the board walk lifted hats to Beth and spoke greetings, sometimes giving Johnny sidelong glances that ran from faint surprise to startled amazement. No man gave them more than custom demanded, but no man blocked their path. Feeling out the town's temper, Tracy sensed that Spurlock still waited, holding to a sort of neutrality and reserving its judgment. Across from the saddle shop, he felt impelled to lift his eyes. The light no longer burned in Smeed's window.

He saw Beth look up there, too, and shudder. He smiled at her and shook his head ever so slightly.

This was almost the hour at which Tracy had reached Spurlock last night, and he reflected that it had been a long circle he'd followed since. Suddenly he felt the weight of all the miles and all the hours. The hitchrails were again lined, and more riders were coming in. Sally's was doing a brisk business; and lamplight showed everywhere, spilling from doorways and windows to gild the dust. Tracy looked about for Ringo; he had forgotten Ringo's existence in the rush of recent hours.

When they reached the jail-house, Harriman's office was dark and locked. Johnny said, grinning, "Maybe I'd better write him a letter."

Something crystallized in Tracy then that had been made of small doubts and shadowy worries; and he said, "You're coming on to Diamond L with us."

Johnny laughed. "Up at Orlando, it was me who couldn't get my backside behind me. Now it's you that's turned around. Shucks, I can't be waiting here on Harriman's step when he gets back."

Tracy shook his head. "We can't risk it. Not till we know how Harriman really stands. Maybe he's the one man who has chosen a side. I didn't do last night's riding to put you in Broken Box's hands." He glanced at Beth. "Does Harriman have a deputy?"

"There was never enough work for one."

"Where's the livery?"

"This way," Beth said and led them across the street and along its far side to a stable with a wagon lot beside it. The hostler knew the Lovetts. He gave them that same careful, uncompromising courtesy they had met elsewhere; he got busy at once at saddling. Tracy waited him out, leaning against a post, his thumbs hooked in his gun-belt and every fiber of him alert to the town's small sounds.

Finally he asked, "McCoy buried today?"

"Tomorrow, likely," the hostler said, his face blank in the lamplight. "He's over at the furniture store in a fancy coffin."

"Any inquest?"

"Haven't heard talk of one. Most people figger that Harriman will put the death down as a gunshot wound at the hands of a person or persons unknown." The hostler kept very busy at his cinching; he didn't look at Johnny.

"What took Harriman out of town?"

"He rode out last night. I know, because he stables his horse here. It was after Doc Smeed announced that McCoy had cashed in his chips. Say, that caused quite a stir! Some of Broken Box's boys were still around town and they could have carried the word, but Hap said he thought he should ride down and take the news to Ramage."

"But the sheriff came back this way sometime today, didn't he?" Tracy persisted. "Riding with Broken Box?"

The hostler's eyes grew guarded. "I don't think so. If he did, I didn't see him. My shift is evening till dawn. The best part of the morning, I'm sleeping."

"Thanks," Tracy said drily and reflected that here was as much as he'd get from any Spurlock man. They were people cowering in a storm cellar, watching the black clouds gather and waiting for the sin-twister. When the roof was lifted off, they would make their choice, each man for himself. It had been thus in Pleasant Valley. It was part of an old, old pattern that always repeated itself.

"Horses ready," the hostler said, slapping the last one lightly.

That was when some warning touched Tracy's consciousness. His questions asked, he'd stood lost in thought, his inherent wariness blunted; and thus he realized only vaguely that wisps of hay fluttered down from a crack in the loft's flooring. This carried no significance that really reached through to him. It was in the very instant that he realized someone must be above that Johnny shouted, *"Watch out!"*

Tracy lunged sidewards just as a gun spoke through that overhead crack. Thunder filled the stable, the lamp guttered from the concussion and nearly went out, and some of the horses began pitching in their stalls. But the bullet thunked into the spongy underfooting of the floor.

Tracy leaped toward the ladder leading to the loft. He had no thought in him save that Beth stood in danger as long as that gun above could speak. He swarmed up the ladder and through the opening into the loft, a heady anger making him reckless. He saw a dim figure in the gloom, a deeper darkness against the darkness of piled hay. He made for that figure, scuttling across the shaky floor on hands and knees. Again the gun spoke, seeming to explode almost in his face. But Tracy's daring had unnerved the one who fired, and the shot missed.

Tracy catapulted himself upon that dim shape, reaching

for the fellow's right wrist and twisting hard. He bore the other down into the hay and pinned him there, the gunman cursing him in a shrill, remembered voice. Only then did Tracy realize that he had closed with Herb. He smashed a fist at Herb's jaw; and the fight went out of Herb, though consciousness was still in him.

Below, Johnny was shouting, "Clint! Are you all right?"

Tracy gasped out, "Got him!" and wrenched the gun from Herb's fingers. He got a hold on Herb's collar and dragged him to a stand; he propelled Herb to the opening and forced him upon the ladder. "Grab him as he comes down, Johnny," Tracy ordered, and letting go of Herb, set his own boots to the ladder. He came to the barn floor to find Herb writhing blindly in the grasp of Johnny.

Tracy took hold of the Broken Box boy and flung him against a wall. Herb sagged to his knees, then struggled back to a stand. For a moment he stood defiant, his pasty face wild, his slack mouth twisted in a grimace of fury. Then he slumped onto a box. He buried his face in his hands, huge sobs shaking him.

The hostler had quieted the frightened horses. He stood staring, his face shining with an oily film of sweat. "On a stack of Bibles," he said hoarsely, "I never knew anybody was up there. Believe me!"

Tracy's chest heaved from exertion, and his wounded shoulder throbbed. He looked at Johnny and saw the anger in Johnny's eyes; he looked at Beth; she was the coolest one here. He glared down at Herb. "So it was to be a back-shooting! What the hell am I going to do with you, Herb?"

Johnny tipped his head in the direction of the doorway. "Doesn't sound like the shots are fetching anybody," he said. "Clint, here's the answer to a prayer. You want to know why Harriman is riding with Broken Box? This jigger can tell you that and more besides." He took a step toward Herb. "What's Ramage scheming, damn you?"

Herb looked up, defiance again on his face; and Tracy

saw then where the boy's pride lay. "You'll get nothing out of me!"

Johnny raised his hand. "We'll cuff it out of you! Clint, let's you and me work him over."

Tracy was tempted. He still trembled with anger, and he had only contempt for Herb, yet at this moment he pitied the youngster more than he hated him. Herb was now revealed, his sorry ambition standing naked, for Herb's real defiance had come when Ramage's name was mentioned. A different hero in the kid's life might have fashioned a different Herb, but it was Tracy's thought that it was too late. From this came Tracy's compassion, so he said, "No, Johnny. There's two of us and only one of him. I don't think we'd be proud of making him talk."

"Hell," Johnny said in a disgusted voice, "do you think Broken Box would figure that way if the tables were turned? If two against one sits hard with you, Clint, go take a walk up the street and back. I'll handle him myself."

Beth broke her silence. "Leave him alone, Johnny."

Tracy still held Herb's gun. He broke open the six-shooter and jacked the bullets from it, flinging these aside and letting the empty gun drop to the floor. He gave it a kick that sent it sliding. "Open the door," he ordered the hostler and stepped up to saddle. Johnny and Beth also rose to leather, Johnny giving Herb a last black glance. The three bobbed under the open doorway and into the street.

They were hungry, all of them. When they passed Sally's, the restaurant's light was an invitation, the restaurant's smell a lure; but Tracy knew they didn't dare tarry longer and said so. The freight had made far better time than horses could; but Broken Box might be moving steadily westward, hurrying its force along the railroad tracks to town. The three had already used up some of their margin of safety. They rode directly south, running their horses until the town was well behind them, then slowing to a walk. Tracy often turned in his saddle, watching the back trail.

Beth said, shuddering, "I keep remembering that boy sitting there sobbing."

"I'm remembering, too," Tracy said. "What was it that broke him down? Was it because he'd shot at me, or because he'd missed?"

"I don't know," Beth said. She was silent for several minutes. "I've been thinking. Harriman might have got to Broken Box and found them ready to ride. And he might have come along to arrest Johnny, if they caught up with us."

Tracy said, "If that's true, then our luck clabbered. From all the sign Harriman can see, Johnny is still on the run."

She said, "The one thing that counts with me is that Johnny was willing to surrender." She became thoughtful again, and finally she said, "You didn't owe Diamond L this much, not for one night under our roof." She turned and looked directly at him. "Tell me, Clint. Why have you bought into our troubles?"

He thought of Corb Blount. "I wondered when you'd ask that."

She said, "Don't make me ashamed of myself. I'm remembering what you said about the burning house and the man with the bucket."

Tracy shrugged. "A man rides most of his days, Beth. But there has to be some meaning to it, or there comes a morning when he asks himself just where it is he's going and what he aims to do when he gets there, because the fun has gone out of just riding."

Beth said, "I'm not sure that really answers my question."

He looked at her in the starshine, knowing he had given her only half a truth and having a temptation to tell her all of it. But as he looked, he found her eyes warm upon him, her smile gentle; and he wanted to hold this moment as it was. No campfire dreaming had ever brought him anything like the bright beauty that was hers. He hadn't the courage to make her think less of him. The sense of his own deceitfulness grew so strong that he forced himself to shrug and abruptly changed the subject. "I've been thinking, too," he siad. "Johnny didn't shoot Hugh McCoy. Then who did?"

Beth said, "How can you be so sure Johnny didn't do it?"

"He'd have bragged about it in Orlando. Wouldn't you, Johnny?"

The boy had been riding slightly ahead of them. He turned in his saddle. "Hell, yes."

Tracy said, "Last night I slipped into Doc Smeed's for a look at Hugh McCoy. I wanted to know what kind of man he was. His face didn't tell me much. He was too far gone."

"Hugh McCoy would have spit in a grizzly's eye," Beth said. "He was a hard man and a ruthless one. Still, all his fighting was out where people could see. You had to say that for Hugh. Sometimes I've thought that Ramage was really the one behind the trouble. He believes in Broken Box as Corb Blount believes in Diamond L, with this difference: Luke Ramage is personally ambitious."

"Then maybe Ramage shot McCoy."

Beth gave him a startled look. "I've never thought of that."

"McCoy got any kin?"

"Not that I've ever heard of."

"Then Broken Box is probably as good as Ramage's now," Tracy observed. "The bullet that downed McCoy made it so. And that same bullet has given Ramage the right to push a fight against Diamond L because of Johnny's threat against McCoy. It would have been a good stroke for Ramage."

Beth nodded. "That's so, And *somebody* shot McCoy."

Tracy looked up. They had been following along the Thief, the trail gradually bringing them nearer the river. "Isn't that the ford ahead?"

"Yes, Beth said.

Tracy ceased talking then and turned doubly wary, mindful that Broken Box might have stationed men here, too, shutting off this road to Diamond L. He'd not been able to count the men who'd waited beside the railroad track, and he had no true idea of Broken Box's full strength. There'd been two at the Notch; possibly such guards had been recalled for other work. At least a couple must have been left with the beef gather. How far then had Broken Box spread itself? He glanced at Johnny and saw that the boy sat rigid in his saddle. Johnny, too, was wary of ambush.

But when they came abreast of the ford, the night stayed placid around them. If guns waited on the far bank, those guns were silent. Tracy reflected that now indeed he and Beth had finished out a full circle, for at this spot last night they had begun their journey into danger.

They came into Diamond L's yard before midnight. Again lamplight showed in the ranch-house, and the dog barked his greeting. But when they put up their horses, the corral was empty save for Tracy's own mount and one other. The bunkhouse stood silent and dark. Tracy peered at the second horse, trying to read its brand, then judged that it was Cappy Lovett's. He supposed that a mount was always kept ready for Lovett, even though the man did no riding these days. That empty bunkhouse disturbed Tracy mightily.

Johnny said, "Looks like Corb took the crew and rode after us."

Tracy said, "Then we can hope that he doesn't run into Broken Box." His concern sharpened with the remembrance of Blount's unbending way.

"Dad must have sent him," Beth said.

They walked across the yard and into the house to where the overhanging lamp burned in the parlor. And here the only man on Diamond L awaited them, slouched down in the green plush chair, a discarded newspaper on the floor beside him—a man who grinned at them.

"Howdy," said Ringo.

This caught Tracy off balance, leaving him mute for a moment. Not even Herb's attempted bushwhack in the livery stable had stunned him as this did. "What the hell are *you* doing here?" he demanded.

"My business is with Cappy Lovett."

Beth's glance ran swiftly about the room and back to Ringo. "Where is my father?"

Ringo shrugged. "I rode here in mid-morning. They told me that Cappy Lovett was off the place. He'd gone riding."

Beth said, "But he hasn't been riding in months!"

Johnny took a hipshot stand that barred the doorway, eyeing Ringo in a manner that was both remote and ready. "That your horse in the corral?"

"I was told to put it there. By Blount, your foreman. He took the crew out around noon. He said I might as well wait here to do my business with Lovett. He thought Lovett would show back soon. But he hasn't."

"All right," Tracy said, wanting an end to this. "Just what *is* your business?"

Ringo stood up, making a tall, angular shape. He had the same show of high good humor about him with which he'd greeted Tracy in Spurlock; he was taking his own peculiar delight in the moment and drawing it out. "Why, I've come to work for Diamond L," he said.

Tracy said, "Then you can climb on that horse and ride out!"

Beth asked, "You know this man, Clint?"

"Yes," Tracy said. "I know him."

Ringo's eternal grin grew broader. "My name is Ringold, though most people shorten it to Ringo," he said. "You must be Beth Lovett, and this would be Johnny. You see, I know all about you. I'm a good friend of Tripp's."

"Tripp!" Johnny cried and took a step forward.

"We worked for the same outfit down south—Tripp as riding boss, me a a hired hand. Tripp showed me a letter he'd got from your father—a letter saying that trouble was brewing up here and Tripp was needed at home. But Tripp couldn't leave—he had a big job on his hands. He asked me to come instead."

He looked at Tracy, his eyes devils that laughed at Tracy, saying, *Tell them different, mister! Tell them different, if you dare!*

Hot anger fanned through Tracy; he knew only one answer to Ringo's unspoken challenge, and that was a violent one. "Now, see here—!" he said.

"Am I lying?" Ringo asked.

"You know you are!"

"I think these Lovetts will want proof."

Johnny said suddenly, "What was that—?" His face sharpened with interest; and he raised his hand, compelling them to silence.

They all listened. They stood rooted, their ears strained; and then the sound that had caught Johnny's attention reached through the night and through the walls and was plain to hear, a muted murmur that grew louder and louder until it was unmistakable.

Ringo said blandly, "Sounds like cattle—a lot of cattle, coming this way."

"Cattle!" Beth cried. "Who'd be moving cattle onto Diamond L? Clint—"

But because he thought he knew, Tracy had already turned and was running through the doorway, a sense of calamity overwhelming him.

11. Winchester Cut

OUT OF the north the cattle came, over the same trail that had brought Beth and Johnny and Tracy to the ranch. And Tracy, running into the yard to stand peering, saw the cattle first as massed darkness. Then he made out the higher silhouettes of riders; and not yet being sure who they were, he ran in their direction with his gun in his hand. The cattle were a writhing, heaving movement in the distance, their bawling a disturbance in the night. The popping of rope ends, the angry shouting at bunch-quitters, the constant hi-yi-ing, added to the bedlam. There were perhaps a hundred head of cattle—Tracy could only guess about that—and a half dozen men hazing them, more than enough for the job.

The herd came straight at the Diamond L buildings and then swerved, moving toward the flats beyond. The stirred dust rose and became a dry mist, a choking, gritty thickness in the air. With the herd swinging, the man at point position rode clearly skylined; and Tracy recognized his heavy shoulders.

Recognition brought Tracy no sense of relief, though he put his gun away. "Blount! Corb Blount!" he called.

He might as well have pitted his voice against the roar of a waterfall. The herd swung on. Tracy got into the corral and, snatching up a bridle, forced the bit between the teeth of his own horse. His fingers were wooden, and he found himself trembling. Not pausing to saddle, he swung up to the mount's bare back and started after Blount. Leaving the corral, he saw that the ranch-house door was open and people milled in the yard. Those would be Beth and Johnny and Ringo.

Tracy was too concerned now with a more important matter to think about Ringo. He rode hard after Blount, shouting the man's name again and again, his voice lost beneath the low, sullen thunder of the herd's hoofs. He knew how futile it was to shout, but he kept at it. Then his presence reached through to Blount in some intangible way; and Blount, turning in his saddle, saw him. Blount moved from point position—the herd was now a half mile beyond the ranch buildings—and lifted his hand, making the circling motion that was the signal to mill the herd and bed it here. Blount cut toward Tracy, and the two met out of the noise and the dust.

Tracy said, "What the hell is this?'"

"Diamond L cattle," Blount said. "Brought back to their own grass."

"Cappy Lovett with you?"

Blount shook his head. "He went riding this morning. I've not seen him since."

"Riding? Where, man?"

Blount shrugged. "That I couldn't say. He headed south."

"Where'd you pick up these cows?"

Blount looked surprised, then gave Tracy a morose glance having no animosity in it. "I don't have to explain myself to you, Mr. Tracy."

The stir of fear gave a sharper edge to Tracy's anger. He said, "You'll tell me, or I'll haul you off that horse! You've been to Broken Box!"

Again Blount lifted his heavy shoulders in a shrug, dismissing Tracy's threat. He might have been a kindly man dealing with a headstrong child. "Cappy Lovett chose to go riding this morning. After he'd gone, I borrowed his telescope and took a look-see at Broken Box's graze from a bluff on this side of the river. It was not the first time I'd scouted their spread. What I saw today was enough to make me cross the river for a better look. Some business had drawn Ramage's crew from both the ranch and the roundup camp. There were only two men guarding their gather. It was the knock of opportunity for Diamond L, it seemed to me."

"Did it strike you that Broken Box was gone because they were on Johnny's trail?"

"That was possible. My concern was with the cattle."

"So you came back and got the crew and cut Broken Box's herd!"

Blount's eyebrows lifted. "Surely you understand, Mr. Tracy. These are our cattle."

Tracy glared. Then he touched spurs to his horse and rode at the herd, cutting into it and working his way slowly across it. The crew, still busy at milling the cattle, shooted at him, but he paid no heed. Bending low for a close look at brands, he crisscrossed through the herd; and his anger made a steady beat in his temples when he'd finished his inspection. He rode back to rejoin Blount, and now Beth was with the foreman. She had ridden out, too, taking time to saddle up first. She was talking to Blount in a low voice.

Tracy said, "About a quarter of those cows are wearing Broken Box on their rumps."

Blount said, "Those who were holding the herd gave us no real fight, seeing the size of the odds. Yet we had to work fast, since there was no telling when Ramage might return with his full crew. We had no time for careful choosing. The cows belonging to Broken Box will be cut out later and returned. Every last one of them. We are not a rustling outfit, mister. Everybody knows that."

In Tracy was a feeling that the whole world had shattered. He had pitted his scheming and his patience and his sorry knowledge of Pleasant Valley against the gathering storm along Thief River, but to no avail. First his plan to block Ramage by having Johnny surrender to the law had failed, for he'd found the law riding with Broken Box. And now Corb Blount had made his threatened Winchester cut and finished off the last chance at peace. Couldn't the fool see that? Broken Box might have kept Diamond L cattle in their gather and gone unchallenged; this reversal of the situation was another matter. Hugh McCoy's death again made the difference.

"You may smile at what some call a man's superstition," Blount said. "But this was a wise move I made. I had a dream last night that augured well for the day. I've learned to trust such signs."

Tracy stared at him in stunned disbelief, searching Blount's puritanical face in the starlight for something sinister, some indication of a craftiness that had its own dark roots. He saw only a man stubborn in his loyalty and in his conviction of right, a man whose intelligence had one blind limitation that made him dangerous to the very ranch he loved. Into Tracy then came a sense of helplessness, for Blount's reasoning was so remote from his own that he could no more reach through to the man than he could reach the moon. Tracy's anger choked him.

"Oh, hell!" he said.

Blount turned toward Beth, his eyes showing hurt. "Am I the foreman of this ranch, Elizabeth?" he asked. "Or am I supposed to answer to this drifter who set foot here only two nights back?"

Beth looked distressed; her face was chalky. "I'm thinking of my father."

"Yes," Tracy said, and was instantly sorry for her. "How about that? Can't you even make a guess where he might have gone riding, Blount?"

"He didn't choose to tell me."

"And you just let him ride away?"

"Cappy Lovett is my boss. It's not my custom to give him orders or inquire into his intentions. Had he been here when I got back from scouting Broken Box, I'd have asked his permission before cutting their herd. He was gone. That left the decision up to me."

"I think you grabbed the chance because Lovett wasn't around to tell you not to!"

Blount moved his shoulders slightly. "The fact remains that he wasn't here to give me orders."

"Oh, hell!" Tracy said again and turned his horse and rode back toward the ranch buildings.

Halfway there, he passed Johnny, who'd grown tired of waiting for his return and Beth's and was riding out. Johnny shouted, asking about the cattle. Tracy spurred on without replying, his mind seething and his dismay a black shadow upon him. He reached the corral and turned his horse into it and draped the bridle over one of the poles.

When he strode to the ranch-house, he found Ringo seated upon the gallery steps, an indolent, satisfied man. There was a glint to Ringo's eyes that said he understood what had happened and what Blount's Winchester cut would mean and that he was taking pleasure from the knowledge.

Tracy looked at Ringo, and all his frustration and anger rose up and fastened upon the man. He said harshly, "Get the hell out of here, Ringo!"

"No," Ringo said. "I think not."

"Then stand up and go for that gun of yours."

"Nothing doing," Ringo said.

Tracy cursed him then, laying names on him that would have brought any other man to his feet with death in his eyes. He used his tongue as he might have used a lash, flaying Ringo and turning Ringo pale; but still the man merely sat. Tracy knew Ringo's pet vanities, his vulnerable spots; and he chose hot words that laid these bare. Ringo stiffened. His face became a hard mask slashed across by a grin turned slack, but his hands didn't move.

When Tracy stood breathless, Ringo said. "It won't work, mister. You want to make it a fight, and you hope

I'll be laid out dead when the others ride in. Because you know what I might tell them."

Tracy said, "There's more to it than that. There's an old man here who sits on his porch and keeps looking south all day long. There's a boy who straddles a fence; and any breeze could blow him the wrong way, turning him into another Tripp Lovett. There's a girl who watches those two, knowing that even though this ranch is important, the two of them are more important. I won't stand by and see you do harm to these people!"

Ringo said, "What you're telling me is that trouble's here. Trouble is my business. It used to be yours. You've got a sentimental streak in you, Tracy, and someday it will kill you. Maybe it's the girl who's turned you soft. That's your concern, not mine. I can see that you ride high on this spread. But can you make it stick that Tripp Lovett *didn't* send me to Diamond L?"

Tracy said, "You've always backed winners, Ringo. The strong side is usually the winning side. There's a smell to your being here."

"You figured I'd hire out to Broken Box, eh?"

Now Tracy saw the whole truth. It was so startingly simple that he wondered why he hadn't seen it when he'd first been accosted by Ringo on Spurlock's street. He asked quickly, "You rode in from the south?"

Ringo shrugged. "What other way?"

"Then Broken Box had its hands on you before you reached the bottom of the Notch. They've been guarding that place, as you damn' well know. Yet you walked the streets of Spurlock afterwards, throwing a big shadow. That was because you'd become Luke Ramage's man before you got as far north as the town. All that talk about picking sides was to have been dust in my eyes!"

"I say you're guessing wrong. I—"

"Don't lie out of it! The first night I was here, Broken Box looked me over, saw I was from the south, and began making guesses about Pleasant Valley. Arizona's a big place, but they had the Tonto Basin on their minds. Why,

Ringo? Was that because they'd already caught one man from Pleasant Valley at the Notch?"

Ringo's grin grew as broad as the whole basin. He looked past Tracy. "Here come three of them riding in. The girl, I'd say, and her brother, and that stiff-faced foreman. Do you want to tell them you think I'm Ramage's man? Maybe you could make it stick. And when you've finished, then we'll talk about Tripp Lovett, eh?"

Tracy heard the movement of walking horses behind him, and gauging the distance they had yet to cover, knew how much time he'd have alone with Ringo. He took a step nearer the man and said in a low voice, "I'll be watching you night and day. Wherever you move on this place, my eyes will be on your back. Believe me. And when you make that first wrong move or say that first wrong word, I'm going to kill you."

Ringo's eyes squinted down, and his grin became only a tightening of muscles. Now he looked entirely deadly. "That makes twice lately you've promised me that, Tracy. Don't be fooled by the fact that I wouldn't fight when you cussed me out. When I'm ready to fight, I'll make my play. And I can shade you on the draw any day. You know that!"

Tracy said, "I'd still like you to try proving it."

"When I'm ready."

Tracy turned upon his heel and cut diagonally across the yard. Beth and Johnny and Blount were just dismounting at the corral. Beth came through the gate and called to Tracy. He turned and said, "Yes—?"

She came toward him, her face troubled. She said, "Where do you suppose he is?"

He knew she meant Cappy Lovett and that Lovett's absence made all other things less important in her mind. He said with a sweep of his arm, "It's a big basin. He'll show back before morning, likely. If you want, I'll take Johnny and some of the hands and go looking for him.

"You'd probably be wasting your time," she said. "There's a lot of territory to the south." But she glanced over her shoulder to where the cattle were being bedded on the flats, and he recognized how one concern of hers overlapped another. The crew might be needed here, what with Broken Box cows in their gather. With the weight of all her worries resting heavily on her, he wished he could comfort her. He said in a kindly voice, "Get some sleep. That's what I'm thinking about doing. Everything will look brighter in the sunshine."

Ringo came striding across the yard, heading for the bunkhouse, a black shadow on the move. Beth watched his passage and frowned. When Ringo had disappeared through the bunkhouse doorway, she said, "I think that you dislike that man very much, Clint."

He stiffened. "Only because I know him. He doesn't belong on Diamond L."

Beth's frown deepened. "If he knows Tripp, Dad will want to talk to him. It would be cruel to Dad to send him away before Dad shows back."

"As you wish," Tracy said, not liking the subject and not wanting it pursued.

Beth said, "I know that what Corb did hit you hard. Corb is as much a part of Diamond L as the brand on the cattle. He did what he thought best. I keep remembering that. And of course there is no undoing it now. Try not to think too harshly of him."

Tracy shook his head. "It's a mess."

He went on to the bunkhouse. A lamp burned dimly upon a table now, and in this feeble light he saw that Ringo had already rolled into one of the bunks. Tracy looked around for another unused bunk; and finding one, he sat down upon it and began tugging off his boots.

Blount entered and stood just inside the doorway, putting his heavy shoulders against the frame. Tracy supposed that Blount, too, was going to bed. But Blount made no further move, and it came to Tracy that both previous nights the man had been in the ranch-house at a late hour. Probably Blount slept there.

Tracy said, "Well, what's on your mind?"

Blount said with no show of expression, "I'm having a couple of the hands hold the cattle bunched out there on the flat. That way, those belonging to Broken Box can be cut out and hazed back across the river before they get a chance to drift. I don't want you to misunderstand what I did, Mr. Tracy. I was concerned only with getting our own cattle back. Broken Box shall have what is theirs."

Tracy unlatched his gun-belt and hung it on a peg above the bunk. "You'll not have to worry about that long, mister. They'll be after their own. Tomorrow, likely. Maybe even tonight. And when they come, they may bring the sheriff with them. Did you think of that?"

Blount's face remained rigid. "Likely you're right," he conceded. "There was no other choice."

"Oh, go to bed!" Tracy said and rolled into the bunk and put his back to Blount.

"I did not come here only to speak about the cattle," Blount said. "Elizabeth has told me what happened at Orlando, and afterwards. Now I am certain why Ramage left his herd unguarded today. But more important, I know that you are a true friend of Diamond L. I am sorry about the suspicion I showed before you proved yourself."

"Then go and be sorry some place else," Tracy said. "I'm tired of talk."

He heard the rasp of Blount's boots as the foreman departed, closing the bunkhouse door after him. Tracy was again alone with Ringo. He listened to Ringo's breathing and tried to decide if the man was asleep or if he had been listening to what had been said. Not that it mattered. Not that anything mattered very much, except being ready for the calamity Blount's work of today would bring upon them. Still, with his mind on Ringo, Tracy reached up and lifted his gun from its holster and slid it under the blankets beside him.

For a long while Tracy lay bone weary and muscle weary, but his thoughts would allow him no rest. Damn Blount and his Winchester cut! And damn Ringo and his sly game! Tracy felt like smashing a table or driving his fist against a door. Anger kept him tossing, but at last sleep overtook him, for he did not hear Diamond L's crew come in to bed down for the night.

12. Trail's End

HABIT'S STRONG hold had brought Cappy Lovett awake early on the morning after Beth's departure for Orlando with Clint Tracy, for although Lovett had sat late in the parlor that evening and slept fitfully afterwards, he arose at dawn. All the professions he had ever followed—cowhand, rancher, soldier, drover, and rancher again—had brought a man out of his blankets early; and so it was on this day. Long ago, moving stiffly in the many dawns, he had promised himself the luxury of late sleeping when the time came that his work was done and he could afford such a luxury. Now that he might have slept, he arose each morning as he had this morning, half provoked and half proud at being slave to the old ways.

Thinking of this, he kindled a fire and made his solitary breakfast and went to the porch. Again habit held him shackled, for he had progressed no farther than this gallery for several months.

Here was his rawhide-bottomed chair, his brass-bound telescope, and his whiskey jug. The jug was nearly empty, so he limped back to the kitchen and found one he'd stashed away and fetched it to the chair. He sat dreaming then, listening to the crows cawing out in the pasture, listening to all the sounds of Diamond L awakening. Sometimes he lifted the telescope for a peep to the south; and this, too, was habit.

His mood was gray this morning, sad with autumn's sadness. He wondered about this and found himself thinking of Hugh McCoy, dead in Spurlock. He shook his head. Many times McCoy had stood with one boot lifted to yonder gallery step, the slack reins of his saddle horse in his hand, a big, grizzled man making neighborly talk of weather and graze and beef prices, making reference to Texas and the life they'd both known. In fancy he heard McCoy's voice, heavy and humorless; and he remembered all Hugh's little mannerisms, his way of standing, his way of canting his head.

He said aloud, "Hugh," softly calling to one gone over a far ridge.

Yet he was remembering, too, that Hugh McCoy had been his enemy at the end. Again he shook his head. He'd never reckoned they'd end up that way, and he wondered how their enmity had come about and tried tracing the chain of circumstances back to its sorry source. His thinking grew muddled and he gave this up. He lifted the jug and had a pull at it, not finding much kick in the whiskey. Maybe he was drinking too much these days. Better cut down. When whiskey began to fail a man, it was a sure sign that whiskey had got too hard a hold on him. You'd think this stuff was watered down, from the taste of it.

Damn it all, something big was troubling him this morning, bigger even than Hugh McCoy's dying, and he couldn't quite put his finger on it.

Presently he heard movement in the kitchen and knew that Corb Blount was making his breakfast. Blount came out of the house a little later and turned his still-faced look upon the yard and said, "Good morning."

"Sleep well?" Lovett asked.

Blount nodded, his face showing a deep satisfaction with some inner thought. "And dreamed well."

"I hope that means a lucky day for both of us," Lovett said. "Saddle up for me, Corb."

Astonishment locked Blount's tongue at first. Then he said, "I'm wondering if you're well enough."

"I've nursed this damn' leg too long," Lovett said. "I want to go riding."

Six months before, he'd topped a rough horse in this very yard and been thrown. He'd had a session on crutches and used a cane after that, but now he was able to limp about unaided. It was during this crippled period that all the trouble with Broken Box had come to a head. But a man couldn't sit forever in a chair; and outside of a little misery in the nights, that leg no longer bothered Cappy Lovett much. And so he watched and waited while Corb Blount went to the coral.

The foreman returned leading a bay gelding, a beast so gentle that Lovett hid a smile, knowing what had prompted Blount's choice.

"I worked the kinks out of him for you," Blount said gravely.

Lovett kept his face straight. "I reckon that was quite a chore, Corb."

"Going far?" Blount asked.

Lovett shook his head. But when he limped into the house to get his gun-belt, he also went to the kitchen and prepared food for the saddlebags. Blount was waiting when he returned to the yard, the shadow of worry on the foreman's face. "Maybe I should ride along."

"Shucks, Corb," Lovett said, "I've been in a saddle before!"

Blount looked to the east; he looked toward Broken Box, his face suddenly hungry. "Any orders for the day?"

"You do whatever needs doing," Lovett said absently and lifted himself to the saddle.

He looked down at Blount's uncompromising face, and it struck him that he didn't know Blount and had never known him. Damned if it wasn't a fact. They had shared blankets and tobacco and all the passing years. They had shared Diamond L and had only this in common: they both loved the ranch. Yet they had been strangers allied, never talking a like language; and they were strangers now, not quite able to reach to each other. This was a sad thing to realize, and puzzling, too. *Hell,* Lovett thought, *I knew old Hugh better!* But he rode out of Diamond L's yard with no worry concerning the ranch, for Corb Blount stood guard.

His trail took him due south; and he rode easily, liking having a horse under him again, liking the morning breeze on his cheeks. The sun stood high enough to have dispelled the dew, but it was a hazy autumn day with little real heat to it. He rode with no destination in mind and no consciouss thought to prompt him, just lazing along. He was nearly to the hills when he realized what had taken him away from his chair and his whiskey jug and his telescope.

It had been there since last night, that prompting. He knew it now. It had haunted his sleep and made for restlessness and done its nameless nagging this morning, persisting like an underground flame that had at last burst forth. He'd been thinking of Tripp all along. And now he was remembering what that drifter, that Arizona man, Clint Tracy, had said last night. "Broken Box has got gun guards at the Notch. Maybe they're waiting for Tripp Lovett..."

That was it! And Cappy Lovett was going to the Notch to see what peril awaited Tripp and to put himself against the peril if needs be.

But to reach the Notch, he had to cross the Thief, and thus he should have gone north from Diamond L to the ford, then ridden south over Broken Box's acreage. He debated about retracing his steps. Finally he neck-reined toward the river and came through the willows to look upon it, seeing a stretch of water as wild as that Clint Tracy had crossed. Fear touched Lovett then, and he was tempted to turn back and give up his plan. He thought of the chair on the gallery and wished himself in it. Damn it, his leg wasn't nearly enough mended for him to be riding around like this!

For a long time he sat his saddle, a little, silver-haired

man faced by a choice. He hesitated, one half of him standing off and looking at the other half until he grew ashamed. He spoke a low, angry oath, touched spurs to his horse, and sent the gelding into the river.

Immediately the mount was caught up by the current and went swinging downstream, fighting for footing. Lovett clutched the saddle horn hard and gave way to fear, the realization strong in him that he shouldn't have tried this crossing. He had known the wild rivers of the long trail north out of Texas—the Red, the Cimarron, the Canadian, the Arkansas—but he'd been younger then; he'd had the strength to battle rivers. Still, some lore of those days remained with him, some instinct grooved deep in his consciousness; and he knew he must hold hard to the saddle horn and trust the horse to carry him.

He shut his eyes. The river's roar became a clamor in his ears, and he remembered the unmarked graves of cowboys on the banks of the Red; he remembered men long forgotten who'd drowned that the longhorns might be shoved north. So vivid was this that he could smell fresh earth and see a tarp-wrapped body and feel the easing of a saddle rope through his hands as the body was given to the earth.

He put all his strength into keeping hold of the saddle horn and feared that his strength wasn't enough. Once he felt himself going over and clutched desperately at the horse's mane, twining his fingers in it and bending so low that the saddle horn prodded his stomach. He was still keeping his eyes squeezed shut. When he opened them, the horse was humping up the bank.

Lovett fell from the saddle and lay gasping upon the grass, keeping the reins clutched tightly in his left hand. He lay for a long time and wished that he'd thought to fetch the whiskey jug along. After a while he got up and groped in the saddlebags for food and ate. Then he mounted again, looked back at the river and shuddered, and rode on toward the Notch.

Soon the hills closed in around him, and the horse labored against the slant as the trail tilted upward. Lovett began riding warily now, not knowing where Broken Box's guards might be posted. But always he climbed, until he reached a high promontory from which he could see much of the basin. Across the distance, the smoke of ranches rose; by peering hard he could make out the rooftops of Spurlock. Again he thought of Hugh McCoy lying dead there. He tried looking for Broken Box's roundup gather and thought he saw the distant movement of cattle, but he couldn't be sure. He had spectacles for reading, and he supposed he should see about a pair for distance the next time he went to Helena.

He climbed no higher than the promontory. He had almost reached the crest of the hills and no man had barred his way, so he decided that whatever guards had been posted had been withdrawn. He wondered if Tracy had been lying but judged not. That drifter had been a hard one, but he had struck Lovett as an honest man. He fell to speculating as to why Broken Box had taken its guards away, and this gave him alarm, for he remembered that both Beth and Johnny were somewhere on Ramage's side of the river. He shook free of this thought. His children could take care of themselves, and there was Tracy to side them.

It was Tripp who really worried him—Tripp, who was so long gone and had not answered the letter that had been sent south. But his pride swelled with the thought of Tripp, and his certainty strengthened that Tripp would come. Perhaps today. Stranger things had happened. He grew warm inside with the vision of Tripp riding down this trail and his being here to greet him.

"Howdy, son," he'd say softly; and he'd watched the surprise on Tripp's face, and the pleasure.

"Now how in hell could you know that I'd be getting here today?" Tripp would demand.

"Just figured it out," Lovett would say.

Tripp would shake his head. "It beats everything. It sure does."

"The main thing is that you're back, son."

This day-dreaming grew so real to him that he anchored his horse to a stout bush, pulled the saddle from the gelding and spread the blanket upon the ground. He lay there, dozing and waking. He let the day drift by, and when dusk came, he saddled and rode down to the foot of the Notch, not wanting to spend the night at the higher level. He had a sharp sense of disappointment.

Again he ate from the saddlebags, being sparing of the food. He wondered what he should do next. And suddenly the full futility of his mission rose up and struck him, leaving him sick. He thought of that letter he'd sent Tripp, the letter he'd so carefully marked to insure its return if it weren't delivered. He counted the months that had passed and made allowances for all the delays, and he knew that Tripp should have been home long before this. Hell, Tripp just wasn't coming! He, Cappy Lovett, was an old fool who had clung to a dream that had been ridiculous from the first.

No, Tripp wasn't coming. Lovett supposed he'd really known it all along and turned his face from the truth, not because he had actually expected Tripp but because he'd wanted Tripp's help since his own strength wasn't enough. It had never been enough. In the past he had leaned on the women of his family, first his wife and then his daughter. But when a man's duty had been thrust upon him by this trouble gathering between Broken Box and Diamond L, he'd called for Tripp.

Now he faced it. He had run from reality until he could run no more.

Take the matter of the bad leg he'd got from topping that horse last spring. He'd been thrown in the past, but no previous tumble had kept him out of leather for six months. It had just been easier to sit with his jug and his telescope, convincing himself that he was a crippled man, than to ride again when riding would have meant flinging the challenge back at Broken Box. It had been easier to avoid Corb Blount's pointed questions about a Winchester cut and pretend not to see Beth when she'd slipped from the house with food for fugitive Johnny. It had been easier to just wait.

He supposed he should now be getting on back to the ranch. But he had small stomach for blundering around in the darkness, so he decided to bed down here at the Notch. Lying upon his blanket and looking at the stars, he thought back over all his years and knew that he had always taken the easiest way. This, too, he had to admit.

Before the war, he'd been a Texas rancher with a wife who'd made his decisions, putting them into gentle language that pointed the way for him but left him his pride. Then he'd worn a Confederate captain's uniform and relayed the order of his superiors. He remembered Jeb Stuart and the hard marches and swift battles. He remembered Memphis and the gulf ports and the long road back from Lee's surrender, the road to a stricken Texas and carpetbag law. Then there had been the opening of the trail to the north and the realization that Texas grass was growing thin, that a man must move if he were to survive.

Again it had been his wife who'd made the decision. She'd come north to Montana in a wagon with the trail herd, toting their three children over that long traverse. She had died in Montana and was buried on Diamond L, and in Beth he had seen her resurrected. But it was a man of the family who must make war, and Johnny was too young. So Cappy Lovett had waited for Tripp.

Thinking of Tripp, he faced the most damning truth of all. Tripp, in spite of his bravado, was equally weak, true son of his father. Because Cappy Lovett had sensed this all along, he had created an idealized Tripp in his mind. But now he knew why he had been driven to the Notch against the hundred-to-one chance that Tripp might be coming today, when at the same time his two other children might be in real need of help. Fear had started growing in Cappy Lovett with the news of gun guards at the Notch. And it had grown until his concern for Tripp had become greater than his own cowardice. Beth and Johnny could stand on their own feet because they were their mother's children. it was Tripp who was the weak one.

He stirred uneasily upon the blanket, sick at heart from his facing of the truth. He sought sleep so that he might be free of thinking, and at last sleep came to him...

He awoke to find his hurt leg stiff and all his body protesting against the unaccustomed riding of the day before. There was nothing to do but go back to Diamond L. He led the horse until he felt limber enough to climb into the saddle. He came to the east bank of the Thief and slaked his thirst and looked upon the waters, and fear was a cold wind passing through him. The memory of yesterday's crossing was too strong. This left him no course but to follow the Thief to the ford and make passage there. That meant crossing Broken Box's land; and that prospect, too, made him afraid. He was a man caught betwixt and between.

The choice he finally made was a compromise that shamed him. He would loiter along through the day, keeping close to the cover of the willows; and he would thus reach the ford by starlight. And so he rode, holding the horse to a walk. He ate what was left of the food and was glad that he had been sparing of it at the foot of the Notch the night before when he'd still thought Tripp might come.

In late afternoon he was skirting the Thief at a point almost directly west of Broken Box headquarters. No smoke lifted from the ranch-house; and he wondered about that, thinking of Beth and Johnny again. Was Ramage hard on their trail? But possibly Broken Box's crew was in Spurlock, burying Hugh McCoy. He wished that he might have attended the funeral, and this again turned his thoughts to McCoy. He had wondered where the trouble had begun between them, and now he knew; it, too, lay rooted in his own inactivity, his turning his face from the realities. A stern stand months ago might have stopped McCoy in his tracks, but he had not taken such a stand. Thus the guilt was partly his, and he forgave McCoy and was at peace with him.

Thinking this, he rode upon McCoy's land; and in the early evening he got to the ford and splashed across it and came into the willows on the west bank. And here he found a huddle of horsemen, a dozen or more. He knew at once that they had heard him coming and were awaiting him. He looked at them and recognized Cultus and that pasty-faced kid, Herb, and George and Snap and all the others. He saw Luke Ramage bulking big among them. He looked at Luke Ramage and saw death.

Ramage smiled a sour smile and said, "Well, Cappy—"

"What brings you out?" Lovett asked.

"Just a few cows, Cappy. Broken Box cows that were run off last night."

"I know nothing about any cows."

"Is that so?" Ramage said. "It sure as hell was your crew come and got 'em."

Then it was that Cappy Lovett understood that Corb Blount had at last made his Winchester cut. He remembered Blount asking for his day's orders the previous morning and himself saying, 'You do whatever needs doing." Blount had put his own interpretation upon that order, and the deed was done, yet Lovett knew no regret but a swelling pride instead. Blount had done the thing that he himself should have ordered long ago. So be it.

"I remember," he said. "It was an order I gave my foreman yesterday."

"Then it's war now, Cappy," Luke Ramage said and was a man sure of himself.

And so Cappy Lovett came face to face with his last fear. There was something about Ramage that told him he was not to ride away from here. But in the last fear he found an end to fear. He sat stiffly in his saddle, thinking not of escape but of the gun at his hip, making his calculation as to how much of a bite he could get for himself while Broken Box was having its feast.

He'd been told that a drowning man saw all his life sweep before him in the last frantic second, but he was no drowning man, for there was no panic in him. He realized that the strength he'd never shown in a lifetime could still be his in this last moment, and he grew bold. He could count on no man now, and on no woman; and he felt both an emptiness and a glory. But the glory was greater.

He looked at Ramage and said in a harsh voice, "Luke, it comes to me that you're sure as hell on the wrong side of the river!"

He saw the surprise in Ramage's eyes—the surprise and the deadly intent—and he reached then for the gun at his hip . . .

13. Death Comes Riding

SOMETIME IN the night an idea of where Cappy Lovett had ridden came to Clint Tracy, and he awoke in Diamond L's bunkhouse with the idea turned into a conviction, just as a man remembering a face comes suddenly upon the right name to tie to it. He hadn't done any conscious thinking about Cappy Lovett; he had been too tired for that. Out of sleep and jumbled dreaming had come the realization, startling in its clarity. He considered the matter carefully as he sat up, wondering to what use he could put his knowledge.

Sunlight shafted through a window and laid a pattern upon the bunkhouse floor. Tracy guessed it was still quite early. About him, others still snored. He swung from the bunk and flexed his sore shoulder and stomped into his boots and latched on his gun-belt. He got his gun from under the blankets, and he rasped his hand across his face; he needed a shave. He saw that Ringo was one of those who slept. Even in sleep Ringo wore a ghost of that perpetual grin of his. Tracy looked at Ringo and shook his head, remembering all that had happened last night.

Someone had left a razor lying in a clutter of odds and ends on the bunkhouse table. Tracy helped himself to the razor, then went to the water bucket on the bench outside the door and filled the basin. He found a distorted mirror tacked on the wall, grinned at his crooked reflection, and gave himself a cold shave. He realized he was ravenously hungry. He'd been hungry in Spurlock, but the tension at Diamond L last night had stolen his appetite.

Across the yard early sunshine spread a dull golden promise; off on the flats where the beef gather had been bedded, a meadow lark caroled. Horses stomped in the corral; smoke lifted from the ranch-house chimney. Diamond L's dog, a gaunt creature looking as if he might have wolf strain in him, came padding slowly across the yard. He sniffed at Tracy and accepted him. Yonder a horseman rode out toward the cattle. Tracy recognized Blount and again shook his head. He walked across the yard and saw Beth come out to the gallery and stand waiting. Sleep had refreshed her and given her a sparkle. He smiled at Beth. She was a part of the morning, the best part of its golden glory.

It was easy then to forget that today Broken Box would surely come; and yet it was the strongest and most compelling certainty in him, blunting the day's beauty.

Beth said, "Good morning, Clint. I'll bet you could use some breakfast."

He nodded. "Another hour and I'd be chewing the heels off my boots."

"We seem to be eating in relays," Beth said. "I've had my breakfast and given Corb his. Now it's your turn. Come along with me."

She led him into the house and beyond the parlor to a large kitchen. He had never been here before. He judged from the size of the table and the number of chairs that this was also the mess hall. Fire crackled in a range, the red glow outlining the stove lids. Tracy liked this room; it was somehow Beth's. He seated himself, and Beth poured him coffee and began frying bacon. She was quiet and quick at her work.

He waited till she had served him and then asked, "Your dad show back?"

Her brightness vanished. "Not yet."

"He's ridden to the Notch," Tracy said.

Fear leaped into her eyes. "He wouldn't have done anything so foolish! Besides, he didn't head for the ford."

Tracy said quickly, "I don't think you need to be concerned. When I told him the other night that Broken Box had guards at the Notch, it hit him hard. He thinks any minute will be bringing Tripp up from the south. My guess is that he crossed the river somewhere and went to the Notch to hunker in the bushes and be on hand to side Tripp when the time comes. But nothing's so tiresome as just waiting. Pretty soon he'll get sick of it and come home."

"But if those Broken Box guards sight him—?"

Tracy shook his head. "Ramage has likely pulled them away from the Notch. If so, he won't be sending them back south right away. Broken Box will be coming for their cattle, and Ramage will want every man at his back. The safest place your dad could be today is off Diamond L."

Beth said thoughtfully, "I could ride down south and have a look around for him."

Tracy frowned, looking up quickly from his plate. "I don't like the idea of your riding on Broken Box's side of the river. Still, it might be best at that. The gunsmoke will be over here."

"I'll stay," she said.

He instantly realized that he'd said the wrong thing and that he should have encouraged her to take the ride. It was a question of which was the lesser of two dangers. He ate silently, trying meanwhile to frame an argument that would take her off Diamond L without costing her any part of her pride. She was such a forthright girl that no guile suggested itself that would not be transparent. Finally he said, "I wish you wouldn't stay here."

She refilled his coffee cup and put the pot back on the stove, then came to the table and sat down across from him, cupping her chin in her hands and propping her elbows upon the table. She looked like a small child, pensive and troubled and wanting to talk.

"Clint," she asked, "what is the longest you were ever tied to one place?"

He thought about this, his mind running backward over the years. There were a lot of places to be recalled. "A year—a year and a half, maybe."

She shook her head. "With me it has been the other way around. Texas and the trail north are pretty dim in my memory. All the rest of my life has been Diamond L and the basin, except for a couple of years at school. That was back East, and so different it seems now like something I dreamed. My real life has always been here."

Tracy said, "Don't you worry. Those old hills have been standing around for a long, long time. They'll be standing for quite a few years yet."

She frowned. "But someone will drag sharp spurs through them and spoil them," she said. "Someone will build a cheap hope around gold or graze, and nothing will be as it used to be. Is it always so? That's what I wonder. A Hugh McCoy dies, and then there is a Luke Ramage to fight. Kill Ramage, and some other man will covet the grass and his neighbor's brand. Trouble breeds trouble, doesn't it? Where is the finish, Clint? Where?"

He pushed back his plate. "I don't know, Beth. I've never known, and I've thought about it, too. I only know that when all else has failed, we must fight. Nothing is ever won for keeps. Nothing stays the way we want it unless it is guarded."

It came to him that he might have been speaking of Pleasant Valley or all the petty wars on all the ranges, and now he saw clearly how constant was the pattern and how there was no escaping it. Sheep or cattle, grass or water or just plain greed—the hour always came when a man could be pushed no further. He had worked for peace here along Thief River and had seen his hopes go crashing. He now accepted the inevitability of this with a strange placidity; he was done with last night's anger, deeming it useless. He thought again of his own mission, the secret that had been a burden to him. Probably a man would always find himself caught up in the chaos of other people's fashioning, but he could still have his own bright star to follow.

But he couldn't tell Beth his secret; so he said, "Maybe when the smoke has settled, we'll have gained an hour or so when we can ride in the sun. Perhaps that is all we can ask."

He lifted his eyes to Beth's and saw that he had brought a measure of calm to her.

She said, "All of our work wasn't undone last night by Corb's making his cut of the Broken Box herd. You saved Johnny from taking Tripp's kind of trail. That's the important thing. I watched him after we got to Spurlock; he never took his eyes from you. He's found someone new to pattern himself after."

"Johnny's a good boy," Tracy said.

Beth glanced toward the doorway and smiled. "Speak of the devil..." she said.

Johnny came into the kitchen, stretching and yawning. He grinned at them both and crossed over to a window and glanced out upon the yard and whistled softly. "Hey! Would you look at that!"

Tracy moved over beside Johnny and saw two saddled horses standing at the corral gate. "Yours and mine," he said to Johnny. "They made pretty good time down from the hills. Now where's Beth's?"

"She'll be along," Johnny said. "You couldn't keep that buckskin from the oat bin if you tied her to a tree." He turned away from the window and stretched himself again. "Sure good to sleep in my own bed. Beth, could you rustle me some breakfast?"

"The rest of the crew will be stringing in here soon," Beth said.

Tracy went to the gallery and seated himself on its steps and shaped up a cigarette. He saw that someone was unsaddling the two horses they had turned loose at the railroad tracks. He watched the Diamond L hand at this work; you could judge a rider by the way he handled gear. He finished out his cigarette and put his boot to it and looked in the direction of the river, bending his gaze northward toward the ford. He wished that his eye might level all the obstructions between here and the ford, giving him a clear view.

He sat for a long time. The crew trooped in past him and had breakfast and came out to the yard again, Ringo with them, the man keeping his distance from Tracy and keeping his peace. But his grin was constant; it challenged Tracy. The crew stirred about aimlessly, having no orders from Blount as yet, the men showing a strained alertness as the morning passed and they waited for Broken Box, waited out the inevitable.

Blount rode in and spoke to two of the crew and they left the yard afoot, vanishing from Tracy's sight. Blount came across the yard and nodded to Tracy and went into the house. Sometimes Blount's voice reached from the house, touching Tracy's consciousness briefly. Sometimes he heard Beth speaking, and Johnny. The two Diamond L hands who were still in the yard hunkered down in the shadow of the barn, moving with that shadow, smoking endlessly. Ringo sat on the bench before the bunkhouse, a man alone and apart.

Tracy got up and walked over and stood before Ringo. "You've had a chance to sleep on what we talked about last night," Tracy said. "Don't you reckon you'd better saddle up and get out of here?"

"I think not," Ringo said. "It's plain from the talk around here that this spread is in for trouble. I came here to hire on, remember. They could use another hand." His eyes laughed at Tracy.

Tracy curbed the hot rise of temper. "I'll be watching you," he said tonelessly and turned on his heel and walked away.

Blount came out of the house, crossed the yard and spoke to the two loafing hands. Thereafter they fetched a barrel to the pump, filled it with water, and wrestled it up the gallery steps and into the house. Tracy gave them a hand at the chore; they put the barrel in the kitchen. One of them said, "You rustle up all the ammunition in the house, Jake, and put it where it's handy. Me, I'll do likewise in the bunkhouse." Tracy left them to their further preparations for a siege and went back to the gallery steps.

In mid-afternoon the third horse, the buckskin mare Beth had ridden, came home.

Supper made another milestone in the tense journeying across the span of that day. The crew ate in two relays, and Tracy judged that those Blount had sent out of the yard had been posted beyond the ranch buildings to guard against Broken Box's coming. Two others were holding the herd on the flat. Blount ate his meal silently; and Tracy, studying him, thought: *At least he's awake to danger.* After supper Tracy went again to the gallery for a cigarette, and he had smoked it out when the wild cry lifted.

Broken Box, he thought, and the sensation that stirred in his stomach was almost one of joy; he was that sick of the waiting.

He stood up. Excitement ran through the yard. Boots beat in the gathering dusk, and a shout that came out of the twilight had an oath tagged to it. Tracy saw a horse standing just outside the corral. Men were converging upon that horse, the two hands who'd been left here and the two who'd been posted beyond the yard. Diamond L's dog set up a frenzy of barking. Tracy peered hard, not being sure of what he saw but knowing the sudden sickening truth in his heart. He went running hard across the yard.

Cappy Lovett was upon that horse. Lovett was tied to the saddle. He lay forward grotesquely, his arms dangling; and he was dead from a bullet hole between his eyes. Cappy Lovett had come home.

Someone among those gathered Diamond L hands said, "Dirty Injun trick! Dirty Injun trick!" repeating this over and over in a tired, toneless voice. Another began hacking at the ropes holding Lovett, and two lifted him from the saddle. Lovett's gun was in his holster. The man who had cut the ropes took the gun and broke it open and had a look. "Two shots fired," he said. "At least Cappy got in a lick." Tracy got the saddle of Lovett's horse; and as Lovett was stretched upon the ground, Tracy laid the saddle blanket over him. Beth came running across the yard to burst among them.

She looked down. She glanced at Tracy for confirmation as though not believing her eyes, and he nodded. She reeled, and Tracy moved to her side, but she brushed away the support of his hand. She braced herself and said in the same tired, toneless voice of the man who had cursed, "Carry him into the house."

She stood unmoving as they lifted Lovett and toted him away. Two of the Diamond L hands assumed this chore; the other two stood hesitating. One cleared his throat as though to speak, then said nothing. Both men drifted toward the bunkhouse, keeping their eyes off Beth. She watched the two who were carrying her father; she lifted her hands in an imploring gesture, then let them drop.

Tracy said, "Steady, girl," wishing she could cry, wishing she might do anything but stand there looking blank and lost and far away.

Johnny came charging across the yard. He barked a startled question at the two who were carrying Lovett and got his answer. This rocked him back on his heels. He was rooted for a moment, and then he turned and ran back toward the house. He emerged a second time; he stood in the splash of lamplight from the open door, hastily latching on a gun-belt. He came at a hard run toward the corral. He had hoisted his father's saddle from the ground and had it hooked over his hip, and his free hand was lifted to the corral gate when Beth asked, "Where are you going?"

"To Broken Box!" he said. Again Beth made that imploring gesture with her hands; and Johnny said, "This is what I should have done long ago!"

Beth turned to Tracy. "Clint, stop him!"

Tracy took two quick strides, bringing himself face to face with Johnny. "In the name of sense, what good will that do?" Tracy demanded. "Do you want two Lovetts dead instead of one?"

"The hell with that!" Johnny declared.

"Get back to the house!"

"Nothing doing!"

Tracy hit him then. There was no plan in Tracy; there was only instinct. He brought up his fist in a long looping blow that caught Johnny at the point of his jaw and snapped his head back and slammed him hard against the corral gate. The saddle fell from Johnny's hand, and the sense went out of his eyes. His knees collapsed. He sighed softly and went down in a heap, unconscious.

Beth moved forward as though released from a trance. She got to Johnny and knelt and cradled Johnny's head in her lap and looked up at Tracy. He guessed that first he would see anger in her eyes and then hate; but she said, "For the second time, Clint—thank you."

His knuckles stung. He blew upon them and made a flat motion with his hands. "It was the only thing in God's world I could do."

Beth said dazedly, "There, a moment ago, with the fire in his eyes and the stubborness in his jaw, he was Tripp Lovett all over again."

Tracy said, "Let's get him into the house."

He knelt and wedged an arm under Johnny, and that was when he heard the pound of hoofs. At first it was only a vague rumor in the yonder darkness; and then it grew and filled the night, a rushing thunder. Tracy lifted Johnny. He got to his feet with the boy draped over his shoulder. Turning, he began to run for the house, Beth at his side. Bent low by his burden, he got across the yard and onto the gallery steps, almost stumbling here. Beth was ahead of him, wrenching open the door.

Then Broken Box was into the yard, filling it with noise and fury and the high, murky shapes of men on horseback. Broken Box spilled out of the night and was everywhere.

14. War at Diamond L

TRACY HEARD a sweep of bullets take the glass out of a front window as Beth swung the ranch-house door shut behind him. Broken Box's challenge was a throaty roar in the night, a mingling of many voices. Hearing this, Tracy thought: *The whole damn' bunch of them!* One voice, shriller than the rest, kept up a steady yipping. That would be Herb.

Those inside the house—there seemed to be several—were a milling, cursing group, caught flat-footed by Broken Box's charge and brought near to panic. One, though, had doused the parlor lamp, and Tracy was glad of that. He heard Blount's voice somewhere in the house and judged that Blount had been the man cool enough to remember that the lamp had made all of them targets. A volley shook the gallery side of the house. Tracy let Johnny slip to the floor and knelt beside him, clutching at Beth's wrist and pulling at her.

"Get down!" Tracy shouted. "Keep below window level!"

"Is that Johnny you toted in?" someone demanded. "Did they get Johnny?"

"He'll be all right," Tracy snapped. He couldn't identify the man who had asked, but he remembered those two Diamond L hands who'd carried Cappy Lovett's body into the house. "Who's here?"

Blount shouted, "I'm here—in the north bedroom."

Tracy got on his hands and knees and scuttled to one of the front windows. Using his gun barrel, he smashed out the glass, then leveled his gun across the sill and sought a target in the yard. Broken Box had ceased shouting. They had dismounted and scattered to cover. From this cover they peppered the house, the guns winking like malignant fireflies.

The yard was deeply shadowed, but Tracy thought he saw furtive movement out by the watering trough. He snapped a shot in that direction and had the feeling that he'd missed. The Diamond L dog was out there somewhere, setting up a furious barking. Tracy heard it above the guns. He was trying to locate the dog when the barking ceased abruptly. Someone else had found the dog and made him no longer a menace to Broken Box. That hit Tracy hard.

He crawled toward the kitchen and had a look from its window and saw that someone was shooting from the bunkhouse windows. He watched the defense being made there and judged that two men were holding the bunkhouse. He remembered the two Diamond L hands who'd drifted in that direction just before Broken Box had ridden up.

Blount joined Tracy in the kitchen, a heavy-shouldered shape in the darkness. Blount said, "We're in for a siege."

Tracy said grimly, "It didn't help much to post guards against Broken Box!"

"Using Cappy was devil's strategy," Blount said.

Tracy shook his head. "It was no accident, their sending Lovett home," he agreed. "They wanted us confused just before they made their charge." He guessed that Ramage had caught Lovett somewhere on the trail and killed him and then conceived the grisly idea of lashing him to his horse and sending him in ahead of the attack. He remembered the Diamond L hand who'd kept saying, "Dirty Injun Trick! Dirty Injun trick!" Tracy thought now: *Nobody but an Apache would do a thing like that!* The thought grew in him, nauseating him and fanning his anger to white heat. But anger, he knew, could only lead to recklessness. He had to keep a hold on himself.

He asked Blount, "Two of the boys with the herd?"

Blount nodded.

"The sound of gunfire will likely draw them in," Tracy decided. "That will put two where they can get at Broken Box's back."

"No," Blount said. "I gave him orders. They're to stay with the herd no matter what. Broken Box may take its own cattle, but it will not take another Diamond L cow without fighting."

Here was Blount's single-mindedness again, weakening Diamond L in its hours of need. But Tracy was beyond trying to understand Blount. "How are we spread out?" Tracy asked.

"Two in the bunkhouse," Blount said. "They're putting up a fight, I see. Two here in the house—three counting me. Then there's you and Elizabeth and Johnny and that fellow who drifted in yesterday, Ringo. He hasn't been hired on. Can we count on him?"

"Hell!" Tracy ejaculated and went hurrying back to the parlor.

Ringo was here, kneeling at one of the windows, his gun in his hand. Beth had crawled to a second window and propped a rifle across its sill. Tracy called to her, urging her to get out of the fight and keep to cover. She made a motion as if to push him away, then levered in a fresh cartridge. He guessed that the rifle was Blount's Winchester.

He looked at Ringo. Ringo fired his gun and bobbed down and began very methodically to reload. Strong in Tracy was his earlier suspicion that Ringo had been planted here by Broken Box, a man inside Diamond L primed to do whatever harm he could when the chips were down. Ringo was going through the motions of being a defender, but he might be wasting his bullets on the dust. Tracy debated about Ringo, wondering if he should order the man outside. But that would only put Ringo's gun against them; here the man was harmless till he made a play. But that meant he'd have to keep watching Ringo as best he could.

Johnny stirred on the parlor floor, raising himself on one elbow. He tipped his head, listening to the constant rattle of gunfire. Presently he sat up straighter.

Tracy bent over him. "How are you feeling, boy?"

Johnny said stonily, "You ought to know. You hit me hard enough."

"Well, Johnny, you've been spoiling for a real fight. Here's one that's big enough for all of us. Go find yourself a window."

Johnny stared at him in the murk and ran his fingers along his jaw. Lead slammed into the room, rattling the pictures of Cappy Lovett and his wife. A bullet struck the Franklin stove and ricocheted; another drove splinters from the organ. Johnny cursed. He took hold of the green plush chair and pulled himself to a stand and made a lunge toward a window and got his gun to working.

"Show yourselves, you sneaking sons!" Johnny shouted. "Come out where a man can get a shot at you!"

Tracy heard movement in the bedroom where he'd slept a few nights back. The two Diamond L hands must be there, and he barked at them, not knowing their names. "Spread out!" he shouted. "One of you take a window somewhere else. Even if there isn't firing on your side, hold your window and keep a careful eye. We don't want Broken Box circling us!"

He heard them move to separate posts. He listened for their guns to speak, and from their silence he concluded that the back of the house was not yet in danger.

Blount came from the kitchen, saying, "The two in the bunkhouse are keeping that side clear." He turned his still-faced glance along the row of parlor windows. Each now had its defender.

Tracy edged toward Beth and crouched down beside her. He had given up trying to get her to take cover. He placed his hand gently on her shoulder and asked, "How does it look?"

"They've scattered about the yard. Between us and the boys in the bunkhouse, we're keeping them from circling the house. But they're moving closer all the time. I suppose they hope to burn us out."

"How many of them?"

She was so cool that it came to him that she had had her baptism of bullets another night. She said, "More than a dozen, I'd guess."

He did quick arithmetic. Two defenders in the bunkhouse. Seven in the house, counting Ringo, who would be on the other side when the last rush came. They were badly outnumbered. Nearly two to one, when you discounted Ringo. The man was a nagging worry in Tracy's mind. He thought of disarming Ringo and trussing him up; he was that mortally sure that Ringo was against them. He was thinking strongly of this when a bullet from outside found a mark. A man grunted in the darkness and toppled over, falling hard across Tracy's feet to writhe upon the parlor floor.

"Who's hit?" Johnny shouted.

Tracy knelt and groped in the darkness, knowing yet wanting to be positive. "It's Blount," he said. "He's bad hurt, I think." He called to the Diamond L hands elsewhere in the house. One came running, and Tracy said, "Give me a hand. We'll get him into a bedroom. Easy, now. I'll take his shoulders."

Johnny asked, "Need help?"

"Watch your window!"

They lifted Blount and bore him away and got him stretched upon a bed. This was not the room in which Tracy had once slept, and he wondered if it were Blount's own. Beth came hurrying in, questioning and solicitous;

but Tracy said sharply, "Get back out there with Ringo. When you get a chance, whisper to Johnny to keep watch on him. I tell you, Ringo is not on our side."

She turned to leave. Blount stirred on the bed. He got an arm up and beckoned, then said very precisely, "Just a moment, Elizabeth," his voice amazingly strong.

Beth said, "Yes, Corb."

"There is something I must say. I shot Hugh McCoy. I want you to know that."

The girl's breath caught in her throat. "I don't believe it!"

"It's so. It was no bushwhacking job; Broken Box only claimed it was. I met Hugh one day while riding. We had words about the grass and the way McCoy was crowding it. He was arrogant, McCoy was, but he was not fast with a gun."

Beth said aghast, "And you let Johnny go into hiding!"

"Would it have been better for Diamond L if *I* had run instead?" If Harriman had taken me to jail? Which one of us did the ranch need most, Elizabeth?"

She said, "You, of course. But suppose Johnny had surrendered himself to Harriman last night?"

Pain not of a bullet's making edged Blount's voice. "I'd have spoken if Johnny had come to trial," he said. "You'll remember that just the other night, when you were taking food to him, I told you no harm would come his way unless it was of his own seeking. I would have seen to that." His eyes were intent, the only brightness in the gloom. "Will you say that you believe me, Elizabeth?"

Tracy moved close and put an arm around her and felt the rigidity of her body and knew how Blount's confession had shocked her. She took a long time framing her reply; and then she said softly, "There was never a moment when you forgot Diamond L or stopped working for us. I know that, Corb. Yes, I believe you."

"Ah," Blount said; and his sigh was long and trembling. "It's best you know the truth, for I may be kept down by this bullet a long time. But I shall not die from it. I dreamed well last night. This is not my unlucky time." He was silent then, and it was a full minute before Tracy realized that he had slipped away from them.

Tracy looked across the bed at the Diamond L man who'd helped carry Blount here. "You heard what he said about McCoy?" Tracy demanded, wanting a witness.

"I heard him," the man said. "And I believe him. He'd have squared for Johnny."

Tracy's eyes dropped to the still figure of that strange, single-minded man who'd been loyal always, in his own fashion. "You're right," he said. "I believed him, too."

Beth said dazedly, "He's gone, isn't he?"

"Yes," Tracy said.

He took Beth's arm. She shuddered, but she was taking this better than she'd taken Cappy Lovett's passing. Tracy supposed that grief ran only so far; and then, like a spent horse, it was finished. He brought her out of the bedroom, his mind busy with Blount's confession and how he might put it to use. Back in the parlor, he saw that Johnny and Ringo were still at the windows. "Quit firing," he told them.

Johnny lowered his gun. "Corb okay?"

"Corb's dead."

Johnny said, "But I heard his voice just a few minutes back." He shook his head; his teeth showed white in the darkness. He motioned toward the yard. "Those boys are running up quite a little account to settle!"

Tracy knelt at a window, his gun poised but silent. He waited till the firing had lulled outside, then raised his voice. "Ramage!" he shouted.

He waited out another long moment, every muscle in him tight. Then Ramage called from somewhere in the yard, "I hear you!"

"Is Harriman out there?"

The silence came down again. Out of it Ramage at last asked cautiously, "Suppose he is?"

"I've got some news for him. I want to talk to him."

Ramage shouted, "He isn't here."

A last small hope faded in Tracy, but he was not entirely convinced. "He was at the railroad track with you."

"He came to Broken Box night before last," Ramage called. "To fetch the news about McCoy. He was still there when we got word you'd taken the hill trail out of Orlando. Harriman came along to make the arrest. He left us at Spurlock when you got away. We buried Hugh and came home to find our herd cut."

Tracy called out, "McCoy's dead and Lovett's dead. This doesn't have to go on. Will you send for Harriman to make medicine?"

"Harriman's out of it," Ramage shouted back. "It's one ranch against another. We're tired of pussyfooting. We'll do our talking to Harriman when this is finished. When we bring him out here. To show him Broken Box cattle in a Diamond L gather."

Tracy asked, "You won't talk peace?"

"No," Ramage shouted, his voice rising. "This is a finish fight!"

Tracy peered hard. Ramage was no more than a voice in the night, speaking from the shadows and keeping himself under cover. But Tracy now fired in the direction of that voice, his shot signaling all the guns to start.

The fight was on again. And in Tracy grew the bitter certainty that it was a lost fight. Broken Box's superior strength would slowly take its toll, whittling them down further as it had already whittled them when Corb Blount had fallen. Sooner or later some of the enemy would get close enough to fire the house. And Beth was here. That made all the difference to Tracy, turning him frantic.

Beth came to his side. "How does it look, Clint?"

"Bad," he said. "Mighty bad."

Johnny crept over and said, "Maybe a couple of us could slip out and get around behind them."

Tracy thought about this, then shook his head. "Too risky, boy. At least we've got walls to cover us here."

"Hell," Johnny said, "we just can't wait for the finish. We've got to clear that yard."

"Yes," Tracy said and turned thoughtful again. Then he said, *"The cattle!"*

"What about them?"

"They came for their Broken Box cattle. We'll give them the whole herd! If we can get out back and make it to that beef gather, we can stampede it through the yard. We'll sweep Broken Box out like we were using a broom."

Beth had moved back to her own window. She looked toward Tracy, her face a pale flower in the murk. "It's too risky."

Johnny gave his gun-belt a hitch. "Let's go, Clint. A bedroom window will be the best bet."

"That's right," Tracy said and turned his gun to that far window where Ringo crouched. "But before we leave, we've got to protect our backs.'" His voice became a bark. "Ringo, lay your gun on the floor and stand up. Johnny, can you rustle up a rope?"

Ringo was a blurred shape, but Tracy could see that his arm was lowered. Tracy watched that arm, his eyes straining.

Ringo said, "You're not tying me."

Tracy said sharply, "I've no time for fooling. I've got my gun lined on you."

Ringo said, "I told you that sentimental streak would kill you."

"Not tonight," Tracy said.

Ringo's voice rose. "Jump him, Johnny!"

"You're loco!" Johnny snorted.

"Jump him!" Ringo insisted. "You blind damn' fools, haven't you seen the straight of it? He's from Pleasant Valley, the same as me."

"We know that," Johnny said.

"But there's something you don't know. He was on the side of the Grahams. Tripp and I hired out to do gun-work for the Tewksburys. Tripp was killed in that Tonto Basin war. And you've all been licking the hand of the man who killed him. Call me a liar, Tracy! You know damn' well you can't!"

Beth came to a stand. She cried, "It's not so!"

"Yes," Tracy said quietly, "It *is* so. Now you know why I'm here. Tripp couldn't come. Tripp's dead. I won't lie to you. I killed him."

Ringo's voice became frenzied. "Jump him, Johnny!"

"My God!" Johnny said.

At last, Tracy thought bitterly, Ringo had played his ace. He'd had his moment of choice, had Tracy: he might have denied Ringo's charge and had Diamond L believe his denial, but he'd been cursed too long by the truth to deny it. And now Tracy, who'd stood in Arizona with his gun in his hand and a Lovett before him, held his gun again and had the feeling of finishing out another circle. He waited, watching Johnny from the corner of his eye, watching for Johnny to move.

15. Thunder in the Dust

BETH DID not speak again. Beth had gone a thousand miles away, and Tracy couldn't reach out to her. Johnny, though, was a terrible presence close at hand. Johnny could be Tripp Lovett come to life; and in Tracy was the devastating thought: *Now I'll have to do it all over again!* Ringo was a crouching cat, wary of Tracy's gun and counting on Johnny, Tracy knew, counting on Johnny's fury. That made the real battle here, inside the ranch-house. The steady, unrelenting guns of Broken Box still rattled lead against the sturdy walls, no one paying this heed in the breathless moment.

Tracy said in a tight voice, "Just ask yourself what it got Tripp, kid. Not the bullet that killed him—but all that went before."

"Don't talk!" Johnny said in a strangled voice. "Damn it, don't talk!"

Johnny was trying to think, but this fact held only faint hope for Tracy. Now was the time when Johnny had to be a boy or a man, choosing a boy's vengeful judgment or a man's larger understanding, choosing Tripp's way or his own. That had been the real fight from the first. Beth had known it, so Beth had tugged at Johnny, pulling him from Tripp's trail. That was the real fight now, but it was Johnny's fight alone. Beth had been dealt the final blow that rendered her powerless. For that, Tracy hated Ringo more than he had ever hated him before; yet it was to Johnny that he gave his sharpest attention.

Outside, there came one of those lulls when the firing dwindled to nothing; and in the silent moment before it renewed its fury, Tracy heard a clock tick somewhere in the house, in one of the bedrooms, the sound a sudden clamor.

Then Johnny said, "Answer this, Tracy: was there a grudge between you and Tripp?"

"He was a gun hired out to one side," Tracy said. "I was a gun hired out to the other. We never met any way except that way."

"Another question: when you came up against each other, was it a fair shake for Tripp?"

"Fair and square," Tracy said. "It had to be one of us or the other, the way it worked out. Anybody in Pleasant Valley can tell you that."

Johnny seemed to rock on his feet as though a strong breeze were swaying him. He became silent, deadly silent. Then he said in a tortured voice, "I keep remembering Orlando. I keep remembering everything since. Hell, no man but a white man would have kept siding me the way you did, Clint!"

The crouching cat hissed. Ringo's shape rose, towering upward and filling a corner of the room with a deeper shadow. His arm made a blurring movement. Tracy swerved sideways and reached out and shoved at Beth, dumping her over to the floor. The flame of Ringo's gun blinded him. The walls gave back the thunder of that gun, and Tracy felt the air-lash of the bullet along his cheek. He fired blindly, putting his faith in the rememberance of where Ringo stood. He knew he would have this one shot and no more. The gun beat back hard against the heel of his hand. He heard the heavy crash of Ringo's fall.

Johnny moved in the murk and bent and had his look. "He's dead," Johnny finally said.

"He was working for Ramage," Tracy said. "His job was to be inside Diamond L when the showdown came."

One of the Diamond L hands loomed up in a parlor doorway. "Somebody else get it?"

"It's done with," Tracy said wearily. "Get back to the window you're holding."

He went to Beth and lifted her to her feet and moved her to a place between the windows where the bullets of the besiegers couldn't reach them. He had his arms around her, but her own arms didn't respond. He said softly, "Beth! Beth!"

She was shaking. She tried to speak but at first made only an innocent sound. Her face was ghost-white in the murk, her eyes staring at Tracy but not seeing him. She said feebly, "I've had more than I can stand."

He thought of Cappy Lovett dead and Corb Blount dead and of the news that had come to her tonight about Tripp. She had got the grief of not one range war but two, and he could understand that it was more load than she could shoulder. He wanted her to lean on him now. He wanted the assurance that she had seen what Johnny had seen, that he was no enemy of Diamond L and had been no real enemy of Tripp's. But still she trembled. She controlled her trembling for an instant, and then it began all over again.

Johnny tugged at Tracy's arm. "We've got to get out to those cattle."

"Yes," Tracy said, but it took him a moment to be recalled to the battle and the plan that had been in the making.

"I've got to go now," he said to Beth and left her and crossed after Johnny into the bedroom where Cappy Lovett's body lay, that same bedroom where Tracy had spent a delirious night. From the bedroom doorway he looked back at Beth. She sat huddled upon the floor, her shoulders slumped. He had the feeling that he'd lost her forever; and though he'd known that this would be the price of his secret, the price he must inevitably pay, his heart cried out to her.

A Diamond L hand crouched at the bedroom window, his gun ready but idle.

Johnny asked, "Anything stirring?"

"A couple of 'em have tried to work their way around here. I've discouraged 'em." Worry showed in the man's voice. "How is it out front?"

"Hot and heavy," Tracy said. "We're going through your window. Cover us till we're out of sight. Then get to the parlor and help Beth hold the windows."

The sash had been raised a dozen inches. Tracy hoisted it higher and keened the night for a moment. Nothing there alarmed him, so he threw his leg over the sill and dropped to the ground. He could hear the guns on the far side of the building; he could see a corner of the bunkhouse. He stood for a moment, intensely alert; his life could hang upon that alertness. His eyes searched everywhere; his ears were tuned for the slightest warning sound.

Johnny dropped down beside him and said in a tight voice, "Easy as shootin' fish!"

"Watch yourself!" Tracy warned him. "Come on now, let's run for it."

Bent low, they scurried forward, staying as close to the ground as possible. The night enfolded them at once and was their shelter. They had got fifty yards behind the ranch-house when the gun at the window spoke. Tracy looked around and could see no target, but a high yell lifted off somewhere and broke in its middle.

"There's one that won't be cutting our sign," Johnny said.

"But they're around here close," Tracy said. He straightened up and began running, Johnny pounding along beside him. Once Tracy looked over his shoulder; the ranch-house had become a formless silhouette far to the rear. Still Tracy's consciousness of danger rode him hard.

Johnny stumbled and went down; Tracy helped him up. "You hurt?" Tracy demanded.

"Fell over my own feet," Johnny grunted.

Tracy guessed they were beyond the besiegers, but still he ran. His breath became a tightness in his chest and a rasp in his throat. His legs ached. The prairie, glimmering dimly before him, seemed limitless. He panted, "Where the devil is that herd?"

"Off this way." Johnny pulled at his elbow, veering him to the left.

Now Tracy saw the cattle. They bulked low against the darkness; closer, they became a restless movement; and Tracy heard the rattle of horns. The herd was stirring uneasily to the distant sound of gunfire; and the two who'd been ordered to hold them were feeling that same tension. *All the makings for a stampede!* Tracy thought.

A rider sighted Johnny and Tracy and called out a sharp warning to the other. Both rose in their stirrups and waited with guns ready until Johnny cried out, "Diamond L! It's me—Johnny."

Tracy got to the stirrup of one of the men and reached up and tugged at the fellow. "Let me into that saddle!" Tracy said. The rider stared at him, his face tight and uncertain.

Johnny cried, "Do as he says, Spud!" He was already mounted.

The second Diamond L hand climbed down, his manner still hesitant and troubled. Tracy got quickly into the saddle. "Get yourself in the clear," Tracy shouted at the fellow. "We're sending the cattle through the ranch-yard. Come along on foot and get in on the clean-up."

"But Corb said—"

"Corb's dead. Now do as you're told!"

There was this to be said for those who'd ridden under Corb Blount's foremanship: they knew how to take orders. Both dismounted riders moved hastily off in the darkness. Johnny was already sending his horse at a hard run to get behind the herd. He snapped a rope-end at a cow; he got that cow moving. Tracy, heading the opposite direction around the herd, got to its far side. He slapped his hat against his thigh and let out a high rebel yell. Slowly the cattle began to move back across the flats toward the ranch-house; and then, suddenly, all of them were running. Fear spread through them, becoming a contagion; and the stampede was on.

This was as Tracy had planned it and wanted it. He and Johnny galloped along behind the cattle, eating the dust they stirred, shouting and banging their guns. The job now was to keep the cattle bunched and headed in the right direction. Yet with the fury unleashed and sweeping toward the ranch buildings, Tracy turned sick with the thought of the destruction they were loosing Damned if he had any heart for this kind of work! He had known war before and found it a rough business.

The ranch-house loomed up ahead. Tracy swung to flank position, trying to string the herd out and work it through the space between ranch-house and bunkhouse. He shouted at Johnny, hoping to get his idea across. Some of the cattle bolted at a tangent, blind with fear. He could make out Johnny on the far flank of the herd. The bulk of the beef, hemmed in between the two riders, swerved through the openness and into the yard.

The guns in the bunkhouse went silent. Those inside understood. The edge of the stampede careened against the bunkhouse, shifting it from its base. Some of the cattle battered against the corral. Tracy saw one wall of the corral go down into a jackstraw tangle of peeled poles. Most of the herd was stampeding straight across the yard, bellowing wildly. A cry went up from the Broken Box men, a stricken cry reaching above the thunder of hoofs and carrying to Tracy. *The hell with such a business!* he thought.

Shadows became substance, moving frantically. Men rose to horses and tried to fight their way out of that tangle of beef. Broken Box was without direction, without plan. A voice rose out of the chaos, and Tracy recognized it as Luke Ramage's. "Stand your ground!" Ramage was shouting. Someone loomed near Tracy, a man on horseback. Tracy caught a half-glimpse of a face twisted with fear and anger; he saw a gun-barrel rise. Swerving in his saddle, Tracy took a glancing blow on his shoulder. He brought up his own gun and clubbed blindly at the man and saw the fellow go down off his horse. Cattle were everywhere, stirring the dust and filling the yard with thunder. Riders cried out in fury and fear.

Thus Broken Box was routed. For a wild space of time the yard was a melee of bawling, frightened cattle and panicked men and horses; and then the cattle thinned out and went bolting into the night. Those who were left of Broken Box had cut their way clear and were riding off to the north.

Tracy had been trying to get to Ramage, but now Ramage was gone. Tracy reined up in the yard, peering hard through the stirred dust. The dust choked him; he cleared his throat and spat. He saw crippled, crawling men, three or four, the fight gone out of them. A Broken Box hand lay almost before him, crumpled and dying. He looked down from his saddle at the man, and the fellow cursed him roundly.

Tracy asked, "Which one are you?"

"Snap, damn you!" the man said.

"Ah, Snap," Tracy said. "This is the third time we've met." He got down from the saddle and knelt beside Snap and saw him to be a gaunt-faced oldster with pain in his eyes. "Can we get you into the house, Snap?"

Snap showed surprise. The anger went out of him, and he was a man who looked at death and was unafraid. He even grinned. He said, "Quite a ruckus we had."

"It's over now," Tracy said. "What can I do for you?"

"Get me a drink of water. I'm that dry I'd have to be primed to spit."

"Sure," said Tracy and took a step toward the pump. Snap choked. Tracy turned and bent over him again, then rose to his saddle.

Johnny was somewhere in the yard, shouting. Two— no, three people showed indistinctly on the gallery, and Tracy judged them to be Beth and the two Diamond L hands. He rode across to the broken corral; his own horse had bolted. He saw a horse sky-lined on a rise and rode toward it and whistled it up. It was his. He changed gear from one horse to the other, wanting a fresh mount and a familiar one for the ride he had to make. He rose to the saddle again, brought his horse about, and lined out to the north.

He thought he heard someone calling his name, but he didn't look back. He knew where he was going and what he was going to do. The knowledge calmed him. He rode at a hard, steady gallop till he reached the ford. Here he turned wary, pulling his mount down to a walk as he approached the river. He cruised the willows first, making sure no one lurked here, and then he dismounted at the ford and struck a match. There were the signs of passage across the river but not of recent passage. He judged then that Broken Box had gone on to Spurlock to lick its wounds.

Something caught his eye, and he lighted a second match for a better look and found blood dark upon the sand. He studied the trampled ground and finally bent and picked up a spent cartridge and another and drew an accurate picture from all the signs. This was where Cappy Lovett had died. His lips thinned down; he looked to the north, where Spurlock lay. Then he climbed to his saddle again.

Riding hard, he cut directly for town. He was a man tired of body and empty of mind, save for one thought. He reached the town after midnight and found most of its lights out and only a few wayfarers on the board walks. But at least one saloon was still doing business. He reined up before the Argonaut and looked at the half dozen horses at its hitchrail. He smiled bleakly and put his own horse among those bearing Broken Box's brand. When he dismounted, he found his legs saddle-stiffened. He stood for a while rubbing them with the heels of his hands.

Then he climbed the steps where once he'd accosted Luke Ramage and walked in through the batwings and found the remnants of Broken Box.

They had the Argonaut to themselves, save for the barkeep. They were only six. Three of them ranged along the bar—the kid Herb; that oldster Cultus, the one who'd first marked Tracy as an Arizona rider; and a third, who was unknown to him. Three others were seated at a table, a bottle and glasses before them; and Ramage was one of these. The two who flanked Ramage had been at the roundup camp that first night.

It was at Ramage that Tracy looked.

The man was sprawled out in a chair; his hat had been shoved back on his immense head; his black thatch showed. He was the biggest man in the room. Some of his hard-driving force had been beaten out of him by tonight's doings; all of his intolerance for lesser men still showed. He was a giant getting his breath before taking long strides again. He looked up and saw Tracy and showed surprise, and then his sour smile came, and he was pleased.

"Well—?" he said.

Tracy took a spraddle-legged stand just inside the batwings, holding them all motionless by the unexpectedness of his entry. This was his ace in the first moment. He said, "Which one of you is going to own up for Cappy Lovett?"

"I got him," Ramage said. "And damned if he didn't go down fighting."

"Snap's dead, too," Tracy said, saying it to all of them but keeping his eyes on Ramage. "Snap and a few others in Diamond L's yard. There needn't be any more dead men. I'm not here to make war against Broken Box."

Cultus' eyes squinted down, a hard kind of laughter in them. "Damned if I'd say you look like a man honing for peace!"

"No," Tracy said, "I'm not. But the big fight's over." He felt Herb's hard stare upon him; he looked directly at Herb, but there was nothing to be read in Herb's eyes. "Now it's man-to-man, and no concern of the rest of you," Tracy said. "Will you have it that way?"

Herb said in startled understanding, "By God, I believe he came here alone!"

Cultus' eyes made no concession to Tracy. "Speak your piece."

Tracy spoke then to Ramage. "It's between you and me. There was Cappy Lovett. That gives me your full measure, Ramage. Tomorrow you'd be talking these others into fighting for you again. That must not be. I'm here to finish it."

16. Beth

HE KEPT his eyes on Ramage; but at the same time he had a sharp consciousness of all of them, the way they stood, the tautness of their bodies, the readiness. These things became very important to him; by such signs he would know whether he must fight one man or many. The barkeep had moved to the far end of the bar, thus showing his neutrality and putting himself in a safe spot. All sounds became enlarged in his long moment of waiting, the drag of a bootsole on the floor, the squeak of a chair as a man shifted uneasily, the sputtering of a lamp. Behind Tracy, the night breeze touched the batwings gently.

Facing Broken Box, he had a growing doubt, wondering now about the wisdom of the gamble he'd chosen to make. He might have stalked Ramage, waiting for a time when the two of them would be alone; but he had not wanted to give Ramage another day and another chance. Johnny had had a good notion at Orlando when he'd spoken of calling Ramage to account and making it man-to-man, but the job was not for Johnny. This called for Tracy's kind of skill. And now he waited on all of Broken Box, just as he'd waited a few hours earlier for Johnny to make up his mind.

He waited, and the silence grew until it pounded at his ears.

Then he heard the kid Herb loose an explosive gust of breath.

To Tracy, Herb was the greatest question mark. He had humiliated the boy that first day in the basin, but he'd showed Herb something of consideration when he'd handed Herb's guns back to him outside Broken Box's roundup camp. He'd been merciful to Herb again in Spurlock's livery stable after the attempted bushwhacking; but he had learned there what manner of idol Herb worshipped. He looked at Herb from a corner of his eye. Herb had a gun in his hand and that fierceness was again on his face.

But Herb stepped back from the bar and swung his gun in an arc that took in all the Broken Box men. Canting his head toward Tracy, he said, "He gets his chance! You hear me? He gets his chance!"

Hell, Tracy thought exultantly, *that makes two kids on the right trail!*

Cultus said to Herb in a weary voice, "Who was arguin', boy?"

But still Herb held the gun. He looked at Tracy and said, "What happened to Cappy Lovett was Luke's doing, not Broken Box's! You savvy?"

Then Tracy understood. Now he was remembering how he'd kept Johnny from using his fists on Herb and how Johnny had claimed that Broken Box wouldn't care about the odds if the situation had been reversed. Since then, something had wrought a change in Herb; and that change had probably come from many things. He had met a tough man in Ramage but a tougher one in Tracy. He had tried a backshooting; and he'd lived to watch an old man die bravely. He had seen the flaw in his idol, and he'd found a new pride to replace a crumbled one. The fierce loyalty he had given Ramage now belonged to the brand Ramage had dishonored. Herb had finally found something worthy to tie to.

Ramage said, "Herb, put that gun away!"

"No," Herb said. "Not till you've made your fight."

The two men at the table with Ramage became galvanized by the same notion. They kicked back their chairs and moved off. They stepped carefully and kept their hands out from their bodies. Ramage stood up, his square face impassive. He glared at Herb, giving the kid the fulness of his hate. Then he leaned forward, placing his hands on the edge of the table. He looked at Tracy and said, "Now, damn you—!"

At the same time he suddenly upended the table, sending bottle and glasses crashing. He fell behind the table, drawing and firing as he bobbed down. He was fast—too fast to be careful; his bullet slapped into the batwings behind Tracy, making a solid, thunking sound. The batwings squealed. Tracy drew and fired.

With Ramage sheltered by the table, Tracy had only the man's head as target. Tracy's first thought was that he'd missed, for Ramage's eyes held him, hard-shining in the lamplight. Then the hate and anger died in them; they turned dull, and he slipped down out of Tracy's sight. Some last reflex in Ramage kept him pulling at the trigger of his gun, but the bullets beat into the floor. Life went out of Ramage, and his gun turned silent.

Cultus looked at that overturned table. "He always did want an edge for himself," he said and spat. His voice broke a spell.

Herb cased his gun. "He had me figured as not much account."

Tracy sent them all a swift glance, testing their tempers. He saw that no man was tensed to take up this fight. He said, "You'd better drift, the bunch of you. Broken Box is just something that got so big it toppled over."

Cultus looked at Ramage and said with no real regret, "That's the end of him." He grew reflective. "So Snap got it. He was a good man, Snap. Handy in a tight."

Tracy backed out through the batwings and came down to the board walk. He felt heavy-boned, and his eyes ached from the hard watching he'd done these last few minutes.

Letdown hit him, the reaction after such a night; and he wanted nothing but to sleep. He saw that the gunfire had partially aroused the town. Lights were showing where windows had been dark, and a dog set up a barking somewhere, and here and there a man stood, peering toward the Argonaut but keeping a safe distance. Hap Harriman came waddling along the street. Tracy waited for him.

Harriman said, "So it's you!"

Tracy said, "It's finished. Ride down to Diamond L tomorrow and they'll tell you all of it. Luke Ramage is dead, Harriman. Have you got business with me?"

Harriman made a swift judgment, the workings of his mind plain to read in his face. At last he said, "If it's over with, that's all a man could ask. Maybe I had you pegged wrong the first time I saw you."

"Maybe," Tracy said, his voice giving Harriman the edge of his contempt. "Only live men cast votes."

Harriman said hoarsely, "I saw you on that freight train the other night. I was there as a friend of Diamond L. Just remember that I was riding with Broken Box to keep them from lynching Johnny Lovett if they caught him."

Tracy said, "I *am* remembering. That's why I'm not running you out of this basin."

He put his back to Harriman and climbed onto his horse and reined out into the street. He came along slowly, done with his work, done with his thinking. He had his own horse again; if it was a Diamond L saddle, that made a fair exchange. He was taking with him no more than he'd brought into Thief River Basin. He remembered what he'd told Beth about a man getting tired of riding. He remembered her trembling with the knowledge of how Tripp Lovett had died. He had finished with his mission, and he'd both won and lost.

Near the town's outskirts, he came past a lighted cottage. A nightgown-clad man stood in its open doorway holding a small child in his arms. His wife stood at the man's shoulder, her hair in braids, a wrapper hastily drawn over her nightgown. These two were peering up the street toward the Argonaut. The man said distinctly, "We might as well get back to bed, Lottie. It's some doings of the wild ones. It's no concern of ours." The door closed, shutting off Tracy's brief glimpse of the warmth and comfort and security that lay therein.

He rode on. At the ford he heard the rataplan of a horse traveling hard; and he drew into the willows and watched Johnny Lovett gallop past, heading north at a high lope. He reflected that Johnny had finally figured out the play, and he knew that the boy was gone looking for him. Well, Johnny would come to no harm in Spurlock now. He might have called out to Johnny; for a moment he was greatly tempted. The sound of Johnny's passage grew muted with distance, and the moment was lost.

Tracy reined his horse into the river and crossed over and rode aimlessly, not caring about trails as long as the way led southward. After a while he came upon a coulee, unsaddled, and hobbled his horse. He spread his blanket in the coulee's shadowy depth and slept upon Broken Box's ground.

The sun was high before it slanted down into the coulee and awakened him. But still he lay, one arm thrown over his eyes; he lay and soaked up rest and was glad for idleness. Behind him lay a closed door and a last step taken; a ghost blocked the way back. He didn't want to think about that. His hobbled horse came up and nuzzled him impatiently; and Tracy said, "No hurry, boy. No hurry at all." The far trails had no real call for him now.

He lay until he grew tired of idleness and tired of his thoughts. He rose then and saddled and headed on south. He saw the scattered remnants of Broken Box's herd; he supposed these cattle would go to the county, now that Broken Box was no more. He wondered who would encroach upon this graze; he knew that Diamond L would never touch it, not so long as Beth Lovett had the say.

After a while he became aware that he was hungry. He pushed his horse harder, having at last an immediate aim. He headed for the Notch, knowing he would not eat again until he was over the hills and had found a ranch on another range.

In late afternoon the trail began lifting and the timber closed around him; and he took to looking for the place where Herb had waylaid him. He rode along in the hills' silence and came around a turn to find Beth sitting a saddle in this solitude.

He drew rein, startled. Because his reasoning told him that it could not be otherwise, he said, "You've been waiting here. You crossed Broken Box sometime today to head me off."

She said, "I thought I'd missed you till I heard your horse on my backtrail. You pointed out to Dad once that there were only two ways in or out—by train, or over the Notch. You are a riding man, Clint."

He shrugged. "Always finishing out circles."

She said, "I have something to tell you. Cultus came to Diamond L this morning with the rest of Broken Box's crew. He left them on the flats and came to our house with his hat in his hand. He told me a strange thing. He said that since Hugh McCoy had no kith or kin, Hugh once promised him that Broken Box would go to him. Cultus had no writing to prove it, but he'd talked to Harriman last night. Hap was willing to take Cultus' word for it. So am I."

Tracy lifted his brows. "Then Cultus had owned Broken Box ever since McCoy died."

"But he didn't dare tell Ramage so. You see, Ramage had spoken to him of his ambition, and he was afraid of Ramage. Now Cultus wants to take over the spread, keeping what's left of the old crew. He wanted to know how Diamond L felt about that. I told him to cut out the Broken Box cows from those Corb ran off and take them home."

Tracy thought of Cultus, a man too old to drift. He thought of Herb, who had found Broken Box something to believe in. The old and the young, they had felt Ramage's shadow; but he had lifted that shadow from them. He thought of what Beth had done today in being generous to the fallen enemy; it had held the same farsightedness that had governed her from the first. This reflection made him humble; and he said, "You've been the wise one always."

He supposed she had finished what she'd come to tell him, and he jogged his horse and neck-reined it to pass her.

She said in a voice so casual as to be almost indifferent, "Isn't the basin big enough for you? Or would the walls shut you in?"

"No, it would be Tripp Lovett I would find everywhere."

A shadow crossed her face. Her expressive eyes held that shadow and showed pain. She said, "Would you tell me how it happened?"

"Ringo told you the straight of it," he said. "Tripp was on one side; I was on the other. We came face to face in a dry arroyo. It was one of those things where a moment's talk, a moment's thinking might have made the difference. As it was, there was nothing but guns."

Beth said intently, "But he must have told you about us. Somebody did."

The memory was so painful that Tracy made his voice wooden. "He tried to say something as he lay dying. Something about a letter. He made a move toward a pocket. I thought he wanted me to look, so I did. I found a letter that had caught up with him. Cappy Lovett's letter."

He saw that she was strangely eager. "And when you read that letter, you decided to come in Tripp's place?" she asked. "Was that it? He hadn't cared enough about the letter, or he'd have started riding north the moment he got it. He never cared about anybody but Tripp. I was not fooled by him as Dad was. Yet I'm glad to know that at the end, he thought of the letter."

Tracy said, "I read that letter. Afterwards I destroyed it, but I couldn't rub it out of my mind. And I couldn't rub Tripp out of my mind. There had been a lot of shooting under the Tonto rim. But this was different, this coming face to face and watching the man die and knowing that the only difference between us was that he took one man's pay and I took another's. That's when the riding went sour. The thought grew in me that maybe if I came up here and did Tripp's chores for him, I'd quit seeing his eyes in the night."

She asked softly, "Was that all?"

"No," he said. "There was a picture. I didn't dare fetch it north for fear it might be found on me here, but I never forgot it. A picture Cappy Lovett had put in with the letter, thinking Tripp might want to have it."

"I remember," she said. "A traveling fellow came through, taking pictures. I'd just come in from riding and my hair was all blown."

He said, "That's what I liked—the free, wild look of you. That's what I couldn't forget."

"Then why are you riding away, Clint?"

He said, "You are always going to be remembering how it was that Tripp Lovett died."

"No, Clint," she said. "I'm always going to be remembering what you did for Johnny Lovett. Don't you think you made things balance? If you are around, Johnny's shadow is going to keep growing to look more like yours. There is Tripp's wildness in him, and it was the wildness that really killed Tripp. But Johnny can be kept to your kind of trail."

Tracy said, "You'll have no more trouble. Johnny will take out his wildness on a horse that needs breaking or on a tough day's riding."

She said reflectively, "Yes, that's so. There'll be no more trouble because you have driven the trouble from along Thief River. But there's me. You said that perhaps when the fight was over, there'd be an hour to ride in the sun. I think there'll be many years like that, for we'll guard what we've won. I wish you'd be here to ride with me, Clint."

He looked at her, not quite believing, not daring to believe. He said then, "Is that what brought you riding after me?"

She raised her eyes and met his with complete honesty, and this honesty was her offering. "Yes, Clint," she said.

He jogged his horse, bringing it closer to hers. He thought of that man and wife he'd seen in Spurlock last night, the two who'd closed a door on all the troubles of the world; and he knew then what it was that had always been denied him. He said, "I have known you for a very long time, Beth, ever since I saw your picture. I have wanted you all that time."

He looked at her, and in her face he saw his own eagerness and his own desire. He opened his arms to her, and she leaned into them. He kissed her; her lips were clean and sweet against his, and there was no ghost between them and never would be. This he knew, and he was done now with wandering; the only trail for them would be the trail to home....

CHANCE

The Maverick with the Winning Hand

A blazing new series of Western excitement featuring a high-rolling rogue with a thirst for action!

by Clay Tanner

CHANCE   75160-7/$2.50US/$3.50Can
Introducing Chance—a cool-headed, hot-blooded winner—who knows what he wants and how to get it!

CHANCE #2   75161-5/$2.50US/$3.50Can
Riverboat Rampage—From ghostly spirits on the river to a Cajun beauty who's ready and willing to stoke up big trouble, Chance is the man women love and varmints love to hate!

CHANCE #3   75162-3/$2.50US/$3.50Can
Dead Man's Hand—Framed for murder, the gambling man breaks out of jail and in a fast shuffle heads upriver to settle the score.

CHANCE #4   75163-1/$2.50US/$3.50Can
Gambler's Revenge—His riverboat stolen—all nice and legal—Chance had to look for justice outside the courtroom...if he wanted the *Wild Card* back!

Buy these books at your local bookstore or use this coupon for ordering:

Avon Books, Dept BP, Box 767, Rte 2, Dresden, TN 38225
Please send me the book(s) I have checked above. I am enclosing $_____
(please add $1.00 to cover postage and handling for each book ordered to a maximum of three dollars). *Send check or money order*—no cash or C.O.D.'s please. Prices and numbers are subject to change without notice. Please allow six to eight weeks for delivery.

Name _____
Address _____
City _____ State/Zip _____

CHANCE 4/87

WORLD WAR II
Edwin P. Hoyt

BOWFIN   **69817-X/$3.50 US/$4.50 Can**

An action-packed drama of submarine-chasing life destroyers, tracking convoys, and dodging patrol ships laden with depth charges.

THE MEN OF THE GAMBIER BAY   **55806-8/$3.50 US/$4.75 Can**

Based on actual logs and interviews with surviving crew members, this is a powerful account of battle and desperate survival at sea, the story of the only U.S. aircraft carrier to be sunk by naval gunfire in World War II.

STORM OVER THE GILBERTS: **63651-4/$3.50 US/$4.50 Can**
War in the Central Pacific: 1943

The dramatic reconstruction of the bloody battle over the Japanese-held Gilbert Islands which the U.S. won after a week of heavy fighting that generated more casualties than the battle of Guadalcanal.

TO THE MARIANAS: **65839-9/$3.50 US/$4.95 Can**
War in the Central Pacific: 1944

The Allies push toward Tokyo in America's first great amphibious operation of World War II, the drive northward through the Pacific to capture the Japanese strongholds on the Marshall and Mariana Islands.

CLOSING THE CIRCLE: **67983-8/$3.50 US/$3.95 Can**
War in the Pacific: 1945

Drawn from official American and Japanese sources, is a behind-the-scenes look at the military and political moves that brought the Japanese to final surrender in the last sixty days of action in the Pacific.

McCAMPBELL'S HEROES   **68841-7/$3.75**

A stirring account of the daring fighter pilots, led by Captain David McCampbell, of Air Group Fifteen as they spearheaded the American drive to regain control of the Pacific.

ALL BOOKS ILLUSTRATED
WITH MAPS AND ACTION PHOTOGRAPHS

AVON PAPERBACKS

Buy these books at your local bookstore or use this coupon for ordering:

Avon Books, Dept BP, Box 767, Rte 2, Dresden, TN 38225
Please send me the book(s) I have checked above. I am enclosing $_____
(please add $1.00 to cover postage and handling for each book ordered to a maximum of three dollars). Send check or money order—no cash or C.O.D.'s please. Prices and numbers are subject to change without notice. Please allow six to eight weeks for delivery.

Name _____

Address _____

City _____ State/Zip _____

Hoyt 11 86